"I find it hard to express how much pure enjoyment and fun I got out of this slim volume."

Dave Truesdale - Tangent Online

Other Work by Ron Collins

Stealing the Sun

Starflight
Starburst
Starfall
Starclash
Starbound

The Knight Deception

A Trevin Knight Thriller

Saga of the God-Touched Mage

Glamour of the God-Touched
Target of the Orders
Trail of the Torean
Gathering of the God-Touched
Pawn of the Planewalker
Changing of the Guard
Lord of the Freeborn
Lords of Existence

Picasso's Cat & Other Stories

Five Magics

Follow Ron at: http://www.typosphere.com
Twitter: @roncollins13

Seven Days in May

The Greatest Spectacle in Science Fiction

John C. Bodin & Ron Collins

SKYFOX
PUBLISHING
Science Fiction

Seven Days in May

The Greatest Spectacle in Science Fiction

This is a work of fiction. All incidents, dialog, and characters (with the exception of a few historical characters) are products of the authors' imagination. Where real-life, public figures appear, the situations, incidents, and dialogues concerning those persons are entirely fictional and are not intended to depict actual events or change the entirely fictional nature of the work. In all other respects, any resemblance to persons living or dead is purely coincidental.

Skyfox Publishing

ISBN: 1-946176-14-1
ISBN-13: 978-1-946176-14-1

For our forever pit babes, Tammy and Lisa

CONTENTS

Introduction

Pod racing in Star Wars aside, you don't find much science fiction focused on racing. That is a shame, of course. Racing, you see, is about all the things that make for good science fiction.

It's about technology, of course—ask any race team in the world what they are working on and you'll get one of two answers, either an immediate flow of excited discussion about wind tunnels or horsepower optimization, or whatnot, or you'll get a steely eyed stare that more than suggests you're an idiot if you think he or she is going to spill the beans on anything that might give the other guy a leg up.

Racing is about time, and time is something that science fiction people have always found fascinating. Time is the ultimate gas, gas, gas, after all. It's compressible, extendable, twistable, and moldable. Our memories change as we move through it. Science fiction plays with time as no other literature can, while racing measures time in ways that no other sport does. Time in the pits. Time behind. Time until the next race.

Despite all the advances in safety over the past fifty years, racing is still, of course, about danger. And fire. And screeching rubber and banging side-by-side runs. Racing is about playing on the edge of capability, the edge of what is known. This is what science fiction at its best has done since the days of Jules Vern.

And, finally, racing is about people who rise above themselves, and about teams of people, the lot of which—though totally reliant on those individuals—are stronger than any one of those individuals. Racing is about that perfect moment when all the work and tears shed in preparation come together to result in victory. And racing is about finding the message inherent in the human condition for when all that work and those tears do *not* result in victory. In this way, racing is life. And so is science fiction. In fact, science fiction is, perhaps, the most human of literatures. It is in science fiction that one can lift a person out of the mundane existence of the real world and explore the depths of who they are.

So we say to the world that there really ought be science fiction focused on racing, and since if it is to be, it's up to me, we've taken it upon ourselves to create this little nook of the world. We hope you like it. When we began this three years ago, our intention was to add a lap to this race every season—and it seems we've managed to keep the wheels on and the car on the road well enough that now we've got five good ones under our belt. And we expect to go the distance—whatever that means for us. These Indy stories are great fun for us, and we still intend to write one new one story each season, a story set sometime in the past or the future or the whenever.

Will you like it?

We hope you will.

Or will the idea crash into the wall at 200 MPH?

Who knows?

All we can say for sure is that it's going to be straight-out, pedal-to-the-metal fun. And that, too, can be said about racing as well as science fiction.

John & Ron
Updated May 2015

Neighbors on Gasoline Alley

Spec Johnson leapt to his feet along with the rest of the crowd as the oddly exotic Betelgeuse Bug, enveloped in its signature fog, whooshed past the yard of bricks that still marked the Start-Finish line. A hush fell over the crowd as they listened for the synthesized Tom Carnegie-esque voice on the PA system. A pregnant pause stretched the moment before the computer-generated voice said, "Ladies and gentlebeings, that's two-hundred and sixty-two point five eight three miles per hour for rookie Xanti Ne from Beetle-juice ... aaaaand that's a *New! Track! Record!*"

Despite the fact that the aliens from Betelgeuse were looking like the main competition for his team, Spec cheered along with everyone else—every race fan loves to see records fall, and after the whole issue with their bio-strips had been cleared up, there wasn't any reason to think the BeeGees (as the

Betelgeuse aliens were known across the entirety of the world's English-speaking population) were cheating. Yeah, it was new technology, but they weren't doing anything to bend the laws of physics and everything fit in the box fair and square, so it still came down to the best driver with the best hardware.

The crowd continued to cheer as the Bug cruised through pit lane after its cool-down lap, but Spec saw something he hadn't seen before. There was no trace of its tell-tale fog, the cloud of mist that was a result of the built-in cooling system it required for the bio-organic portion of its control system. And as far as Spec could remember, the BeeGees were diligent about keeping that misting system on whenever the car was in direct sunlight, only turning it off once they had a chance to erect the portable tent they were allowed to use in place of the standard umbrellas for human drivers.

With the kind of hot that had mugged Indy this May, everyone's "cool-down" lap was a purely figurative thing, so seeing the Bug without its misting system flowing felt like a bad sign to Spec.

Spec watched as half the BeeGee pit crew rushed to erect their tent and the rest scrambled onto Pit Road carrying what looked like old-fashioned water-pressurized fire extinguishers. They positioned themselves at each of the four corners of the Bug and proceeded to hose the little car down like it was on fire. The crew moved with sharp actions. Very direct. Efficient. No movement wasted. Spec had been around pit lane long enough to recognize a crew that was hiding something, and this crew definitely fit that description.

"Wow!" Spec's teammate Wing Brae screamed in his ear. "What a run!"

"Yeah," Spec replied quietly, still focused on the BeeGees.

Like Spec, Wing was one of Team Venturi's mechanics, but so little of what the BeeGees did qualified as "mechanical" that Wing had a hard time following what was going on in their stall. "Wing" was short for "Wingnut." Everyone on the team got such a nickname, generally something like "Oil Spot," or "Ratchet Head," but there were the occasional "Dumbass" and "Meatgrinder" here and there, too. Regardless, Wing got his name because he was passionate about most everything he did, and because he was given to the occasional knee-jerk reaction to any insinuation that he might be wrong. He got away with it, though, because he was a helluva a mechanic and because at 6'4", 225 pounds, there weren't too many folks willing to argue with him.

It was only when Wing noticed Spec wasn't cheering that he followed Spec's gaze to the activity in the BeeGee's pit stall. Not being the shiniest wrench in the toolbox, it took a couple of beats for him to catch on. Then his brow furrowed and he shouted into Spec's ear.

"Looks like they're having some kind of Peruvian fire drill—what happened?"

Spec shook his head.

"Not sure, but look at the bio-matrix control traces—those lines you typically see glowing that odd fluorescent green."

"Oh, yeah," Wing replied. "Definitely not glowing now, are they?"

No, they were not. In fact, they looked more like dead leaves.

"The Bug came around with no misters on, so I'm thinking something broke on the cool-down lap. The driver looks fine, but I wonder if they cooked their bio-matrix."

As they watched, the "fire squad" stopped spraying, and all movement ceased.

The BeeGee pit stall grew eerily quiet, and every BeeGee eye stalk on pit lane drooped toward the ground.

Spec was no expert on alien morphology, but he could recognize a crew in mourning.

"Seems a little much for a batch of fried of bio-goo, doesn't it?" Wing said, rubbing his stomach. "Wonder if it's crunchy."

Spec ignored him and watched two more BeeGees arrive in their own version of a golf cart, then immediately go to work at the rear of the car.

They opened a shiny aluminum case that looked a lot like a first-aid kit, and they extracted several tools. One cracked the seal on an oddly oversized petri dish, and the other used a tool to peel the rear-most bio-matrix strip from the rear wing area and feed it into the dish. They repeated this operation several times, moving completely around the car as they peeled the strip away.

Once they were done, they tucked the dish and the tools back into the case, snapped the lid shut, and gently placed it into the golf cart, which then hummed off to the garage area doing double-time.

"Whoa," Wing finally said, "what just happened?"

"Not sure," Spec replied. "But judging by the BeeGees' reaction, you'd think they just lost a teammate."

"Weird," Wing replied.

"Yeah," Spec said. "Weird."

"Weird" was a term that could be applied to almost everything about the BeeGees. The initial weirdness had started months before when the Betelgeuse racing team submitted their entry to the Indy 500. Nobody had expected something like that from the BeeGees, but they explained that they wanted to better integrate into human society—to share experiences and grow together. In other words, their first contact process had been bumpy as hell, and they were looking for ways to tidy things up a bit.

And, let's face it, the BeeGees had definitely started off on the wrong foot when they put the entire city of Albuquerque into suspended animation for three days. And they hadn't helped their case any when, a week later, they sucked up the entirety of Lake Victoria and planted trees in the soggy basin that had been left behind.

Those were honest mistakes, they said.

They came in peace.

They thought the folks in Albuquerque were parasites and that the people of Earth would be *happy* to have their reforestation processes enhanced. Please, they begged. Please don't nuke us. Please don't laser us off the face of the universe. Please. It was just a couple of teeny, tiny mistakes.

Could happen to anyone.

Weeks of negotiation commenced, during which evening "sighting" parties became the thing to do. Folks gathered together for barbeque and beer and sitting outside to watch the BeeGees' spaceships cross the nighttime skies in their low earth orbits. Newscasts and viral videos alike were full of the purple and green creatures, and several companies started marketing floppy eye pod stalks that stuck to kid's foreheads.

Turns out the BeeGee contingent were looking for new worlds because their scientists had determined Betelgeuse, their home star, was going to blow sometime soon (soon in the galactic measure, anyway). So, yes, they were out prospecting for real estate, and apparently they figured that even though Earth's school systems were a little weak, Sol was a right pleasant neighborhood with upper-end potential.

As one might expect, this news was about as welcome as a termite swarm.

Mars, the BeeGee ambassador said quickly. They had meant they would inhabit Mars.

But the damage had been done. People were

unhappy.

And so the BeeGees, looking for a way to share something of themselves while waiting for their Martian terraforming operation to arrive in system, decided to be neighborly and enter the world's most famous race.

At least that was the story.

It was mid-afternoon, that time when the track was slowest and qualification traffic was thin. And it was damned hot, even for Indy. Temps in the mid-90s, and humidity not much lower.

Like everyone else, Spec wiped his brow and shaded his eyes from the beating sun as he looked down Gasoline Alley toward the aliens' garage. Unlike most, however, Spec felt bad for the aliens. It was apparent they weren't going to get their shot at the pole—and he knew how bad it felt to sit out pole day with mechanical problems, knowing all the while that you had the fastest car in the field. That sucks, even if you're from Betelgeuse.

The smell of warm concrete and tacky rubber seemed to rise like waves.

These kinds of temps can do terrible things to rubber, plastics, and other composites that have a tendency to go gooey, and all the talk throughout the garage was that Xanti Ne's engineers hadn't designed for this kind of heat. It was a mistake that had reporters and fans alike laughing.

"No alien can just waltz into Indy and expect to do much the first time," Makenzie Palli said during a live trackside interview right after the rumors that the Betelgeuse team was flailing around had started to circulate. The fans cheered and nodded.

Palli was an Indy crowd fave, a woman with a cult following: beautiful on the red carpet, fast on the track, and competitive to the bone. She had won the last two 500s, and pretty much had her pick of rides. But Xanti Ne and his Betelgeuse Bug's last practice lap had made the alien an immediate threat, and that made the true dyed-in-the-wool fans unhappy.

It is the way of fans to love the past and hold onto the present, after all.

They didn't take to rear engine cars back in the day, either, and they struggled with the whooshing of turbine power to the point that executives in charge banned the engines after a couple years. Beyond the technological aspect of change, as a few of the more touchy-feely zines had been reporting—the core of Indy fandom hadn't really liked foreign *drivers* either, until the likes of Jimmy Clark, Graham Hill, and Jackie Stewart made their pilgrimage to the brickyard. Though, perhaps the final straw that changed things for good was the arrival of widely popular Emerson Fittipaldi.

And let's not talk about the reception the world gave the first female drivers who attempted to take on the beast that was Indy. The chances of Makenzie Palli even getting a ride in the 1960s or 70s would have been nil.

Things change, though, and merit eventually wins out. Racing culture had been nothing but inclusive for as long as Spec had been alive, which would be 50 years come June.

But an alien? A driver from a star system 640 light-years away?

There are limits.

News of the BeeGees' misfortune sent waves of delight rolling through the crowds, and had planted such a large army of media and hecklers outside the Bug's garage that the team had finally closed their doors.

Wing came to stand next to a tower of tires, and he spat on the ground.

"What are they doin'?" he asked.

"Can't tell," Spec replied. "Doors are closed."

Wing nodded toward the vulturous cloud of media surrounding the garage. If there is one thing pretty much every race team understands it's that the media is the devil's work. "Serves 'em right," he said.

"I'm thinking we ought to give 'em a hand," Spec said.

"The aliens?"

"We would do it with anyone else."

"Yeah," Wing looked at the vultures. "But …"

Spec understood. Helping another driver might be the norm, but Xanti Ne was not the norm. If anything went wrong, the paparazzi would run with it like a pack of gold-digging floozies after bad hook-ups. Lending the Betelgeuse team a hand could be a disaster in the making.

Spec stood up and wiped his palms on his back pockets.

"I'm going in," he said as he strode toward the aliens' garage. "Join me if you want."

"Crap," Wing said, pushing off the stack of tires and scuttling along after Spec.

His friend told everyone that *his* nickname, "Spec," came about because he always worked to specifications, but Wing knew it was because he had this thing about him that caused him to go off the rails and try things no sane man should ever try. He was nosy and he was flighty. He did things that didn't make sense. But several times over the past few seasons his instincts had resulted in victory. So, in reality, Spec was short for "Speculative."

Today, though, Wing figured Spec was short for Spectacularly Stupid.

But Wing was a good teammate, and Spec was a good guy. And, to be honest, the day had been a bit boring now that Jansen Jeniah, their driver, had posted his qualifying time. So Wing followed along as Spec parted the sea of beat droids and daylight vampires with their cameras and recorders and, for all he knew, their X-ray and infrared sensors that would strip them bare.

The combined stare of a couple hundred reporters was heavier than Spec expected, but he rapped on the door, and then, when no one answered, he rapped again.

"Guess they don't want any help," Wing said.

"Hey!" Spec called. "I'm not a reporter. Let me

in.”

This caused several reporters to scowl and scratch their heads, but eventually they all just edged in even closer.

“Hold them back,” Spec told Wing.

Wing was more than happy to turn his attention to something more physical than waiting for a Betelgeuse mechanic to get off his ass. He pushed the group of vultures back by wind-milling his arms and threatening to do anatomically difficult things with the wrench he kept in his back pocket.

“What do you want?” The voice from inside was clipped and nervous like the BeeGees can get. It was one of the things that caused the world pause when the aliens first arrived and said, essentially, “Take me to your leader.”

“Maybe I can help you figure out what’s wrong,” Spec said.

The door cracked open, and a purple eye pod snaked out.

A wave of voices came from the press, but Wing’s glare kept them in place.

“Why would you help?”

“Just being neighborly. Don’t know how the boys on your circuit do things, but it’s what we do down here on Gasoline Alley. Can’t give you no secrets, but Wing and me here, well, we’ll be happy to see what we can do to get you rolling again if you’re all right with that.”

The door closed, voices rattled off a string of strange vibes, and then the door opened enough to let Spec in (and then a little wider to admit Wing).

It took a minute for Spec's eyes to recover, but when they did they took in a spotless office and a spotless garage with the carcass of a Bug chassis up on jacks and with an explosion of parts laid out in precise locations that, on the whole, looked like the assembly directions from one of those old plastic models Spec used to build and crash back when he was a kid. A bank of instruments ran along the far wall—which is where all the gadget boys kept all their electronic gizmos in a normal human team, but these gizmos were more like crosses between lava lamps and fish tanks than electric boxes. They pulsed with blue and red and green and silver. Great globs of ... something ... seemed to float in them, or maybe swim in them would be a better descriptor.

"Are those things alive?" Wing whispered.

Spec didn't know, but he figured he had to say something.

"I'm Spec," he said, pointing to himself. Then he pushed a thumb toward Wing. "This here is Wingnut. We're with Jansen Jeniah's team."

"Welcome, Spec," said the BeeGee. "I am Pennisha Fra-entang ek Abrah. You can call me Penni. These," he said as one of his multiple eye pods scanned across the garage to take in five other BeeGees, "are the rest of the team."

"What seems to be the problem?" Spec asked the Betelgeuse engineer.

"My back hurts," Penni said. "They don't pay me anything near what I'm worth, and my daughter's going out with a guy who's got no future."

"I mean, what's the problem with the car?"

"Ah."

Silence ensued, during which the three of them scanned the parts spread out over the floor, and the whole garage was bathed in a wave of green light from the energy pools alongside the walls.

"Can't you see," Penni said.

"I'm not up on BeeGee technology, but I'm guessing you have a cooling problem."

Penni's body gave a shudder, which Spec interpreted as a sigh. Then Penni led Spec and Wing to a spot beside the power plant. It was an amazing device, part fuel cell, part solar multi-charger, part atomic masher.

"I don't like the feel of this, Spec," his partner said.

But Spec was already down on one knee and peering up into the heat exchangers. He whistled softly at the organic data strip that was painted alongside the housing. That strip was apparently the key to their entire package. As everyone understood from their interviews, part of the BeeGee's technology was based on a living creature, or a culture of live creatures (no one could quite tell), called the Frangio. Spec quickly realized that what he was looking at now was most likely just a part of that biometric interface—the main collective was most likely the bio-strips the BeeGee "paramedics" had peeled off of the Bug earlier. What he had mistaken for a bio-matrix may well have been the actual

Frangio itself.

All he really knew was that the thing(s) rode along in the car like little bio-computers, monitoring everything they touched, and making minute adjustments as the car traversed the course. Need more pressure in the front left, the Frangio made it happen. Drop camber a bit to milk the tires, the Frangio could turn the crank. Add a little wing going into three, or trim it out a bit coming out of four. You got it.

Amazing if it was true.

Biotech computing matrices were still in the theoretical realm for humans, thanks to the Organic Stem Cell Computing Research Ban of '25, which outlawed any attempts to generate organic sources of computing power. Ironically, support for this ban wasn't centered on stem cell research, which was now widely allowed for biotech pharmaceutical use and also for organ growth banks. It was the fear of creating an organic computer that might achieve self-awareness that ultimately led to the ban, and this legislation marked the first time that all the directors of all of Earth's corporate states had universally agreed on any single law (except, of course, for SAP/Switzerland, who abstained).

That left humans solidly mired in the silicon realm of computer processing and, Spec felt, limited in their ability to develop higher-level quantum computing—there was only so much you could do with silicon miniaturization, even using nanotech builders.

At first the Indy rules committee didn't know how to classify the BeeGee's integrated biotech approach. Remote on-track adjustments were a no-no by the rules, and everyone considered it a cheat. But the BeeGees argued that the Frangio were not a technology at all, that the Frangio was another life form, and that the pair of civilizations had merely teamed up to create a sum that was greater than their parts. They argued it was no different than having a mechanic ride along, and that this harkened back to the very roots that the Indianapolis 500 had been founded upon.

So, ultimately, they were able to bypass the Earth's sentient-organic computing ban because the Frangio were a life form first and a computing device second, no different from a human being, really.

Wing nudged Spec, snapping his attention back to the here-and-now.

"That's definitely the problem," Wing said, pointing at the place where the bio-matrix usually sat. "That data strip is usually glowing bright green, but now all you can see is a few punky brown flakes."

Spec rolled his eyes at Wing's statement of the obvious.

"You're most certainly right," Penni replied.

"Can you replace it?"

"No way. The Frangio ... work on a strict contract."

"Contract?"

"Yes, contract, that is your term, I believe. Ten days on, two days off."

Wing spoke up. "You mean to tell me that the only reason you can't run for the pole after setting a record fast time in practice is because your partner's shift is over for the week?"

"Yes, that is what I'm saying."

"But I thought you had an over-heating problem?" Spec said.

Penni gave a total body shake that might have been a laugh—or maybe a cringe? Spec couldn't read the BeeGees well enough to be able to tell exactly what he was seeing. "Have you seen Xanti Ne?" Penni asked. "He's pretty hot about it. But no, we have no problem. And we can still run just as fast as ever if the Frangio come back on line."

"Sure looked like something was wrong after your cool-down lap," Spec said, then he stopped himself. His brow furrowed. Something didn't seem right— the BeeGee's story didn't line up with what he had seen.

"So you don't need help?" Wing said.

"Not a bit."

"Then why did you let us ... " Wing said, but he trailed off as the BeeGee engineers pulled energy-beam rifles from a collection of hiding places.

"Dammit," Spec swore softly as he rose to his feet and raised his hands.

"Huh?" Wing asked, blinking.

"Sorry, pal," Spec said to his teammate. "Looks like I thought a little too much out loud."

"Indeed," Penni replied.

"I think maybe there's been a misunderstanding," Spec said. "We're just here to help."

Ever the man of action, though, Wing had other plans. "I don't know about you, Spec, but I'm planning on stayin' alive," he said as he grabbed the wrench out of his back pocket and commenced to swinging.

Green pulses flashed from BeeGee rifles, and Wing hit the ground with a thud.

"Wing!" Spec fell to his knee to check on his buddy. "What have you done?"

"They were set on stun," Penni said. "He should be fine, assuming."

"Assuming? What the hell does that mean?"

"Assuming we've got the dose right. We couldn't decide whether to hit him with our estimates for a human or an elephant."

"Elephant?"

"Well, he *is* quite large, don't you think? We settled for something in the middle."

Elephant or not, Wing was still breathing and Spec figured that was a good sign. He stood up and faced the battery of armed engineers. Something was wrong here. He saw it in the way their eye pods waved and drooped.

"Follow us," Penni said. "And no one gets hurt."

"Tell that to Wing there."

But Spec knew he was outmatched, and he followed Penni through a door to the back where he found something that vaguely resembled an electric chair, complete with wrist and ankle straps and cords that ran to an electric plug in the wall. A strange shoulder brace circled the chair back, and there were more of the tanks here, too, each glowing and flashing its own pattern of colors.

"They're communicating, aren't they?" Spec said.

"Have a seat," Penni replied.

"If you think I'm going to let myself get fried without a fight, you're just jive talking." He ducked and tried to slip out the back door, but one of the engineers seemed to grow a foot-like stub, and he thrust it out so that Spec tripped and sprawled to the concrete floor. He turned to find himself staring down the cold barrel of an energy weapon he imagined was set on "Whale."

"Okay, I see we're still having a misunderstanding here," Spec said cautiously. "I don't really want to fight, and I appreciate the hospitality, but maybe I should just take my friend and be on my way."

"Into the seat," Penni said.

Spec rubbed his bruised palms as he walked toward the seat. The contraption didn't have the salad-bowl cap he imagined an electric chair might have, but otherwise his opinion was unchanged.

"Why are you doing this?" he said, sitting down.

The chair was hard against his butt. Penni pushed him firmly backward, and he felt the harness snap into place. It clasped his shoulders and pulled them into a position that would almost certainly have made a 19th century schoolmarm proud. The ankle braces grabbed his legs and wrist cuffs locked him down.

His heart pounded.

Crap. This is what he got for being a good neighbor. This is what he got for trying to help out. Of course, it was more than that, too. This is what he got for being unable to let well enough alone. Curiosity killed the cat, his great grandfather had once said. He had wanted to know what was going on in the closed recesses of the alien's garage, and now he knew. Kinda.

But now, strapped into this torture device from a star system far, far away, Spec looked at Penni and saw two things in the BeeGee's multiple eye pods that he hadn't expected.

Sympathy and pain.

Penni didn't actually want to do this. Of course he didn't. Spec knew racing communities, and he figured they couldn't be that different from place to place. Race teams fight each other, and race teams argue for any scrap of advantage they can possibly get. Race teams scream when other teams cheat, then scramble to cheat the same damned way. Race teams respect the code, though. And when times get tough, race teams draw the circle about themselves and they fight for each other, because if they know one thing it's that theirs is truly a business of life and death, that they've given their hearts and souls to the chase for speed and that this chase can kill with the blink of an eye.

And now Spec saw the pain in Penni's face.

"What's wrong, dude?" Spec said. "Why are you

doing this?"

And that's when Spec saw the green coloring at the back of Penni's neck. At first he thought it was a tattoo, but no. It changed right before Spec's eyes, adjusting from a blocky, Egyptian-looking hieroglyphic to a loopy thing like a vine or a thread. Penni used a purple finger to pull his collar back and expose even more of it.

"That's a Frangio, isn't it?" Spec said. "Just like what gets slapped on the Bug?"

Penni nodded. His eyes grew even darker.

One of the engineers went to the wall, removed a tank, and brought it forward to mount it onto a bracket at the back of Spec's electric chair. A mechanism kicked in and the tank started to draw toward the base of Spec's skull.

Spec understood clearly that in less than a minute he was going to have his own Frangio-pairing.

He pulled against the cuffs, and twisted his legs to no avail. Outside, he heard the roaring scream of an engine firing. Someone was prepping for a run. It was getting later in the afternoon, and qualifications would start drawing attention again.

"No!" he screamed. "Help! Get me out of here!"

The Frangio were behind this, Spec realized. Somehow the Frangio were controlling Penni and the rest of the engineers. He saw it clearly now, saw it in every one of the BeeGee's eyes as the machine drew nearer and nearer. No wonder they were so distraught when their bio-matrix fried. He saw their despair as a cold tendril slid over the nape of his neck. A shudder crossed his back, then a shock of cold and a band of heat numbed his spine.

Then nothing.

Or actually, nothing different, except for maybe the fact that he wanted to go swimming.

Then there was a single voice.

"Get outta my way," it said, resonating inside his head.

Excuse me? Spec thought, realizing he was hearing the Frangio via some neuro-hocus-pocus.

"I need to take over the frontal cortex. Please get outta my way."

Over my dead body.

"We can arrange that."

Yes, but that won't help anyone, now, will it?

Spec felt a strange pull to his thoughts, but he imagined himself tugging back. They sat there like that for a long time, each wrestling for control until the Frangio seemed to let go. For an instant, Spec felt free. For an instant he heard only his own thoughts.

Then, suddenly, he felt it all—the cascading voices of millions of Frangio, the links with each of their BeeGee hosts, the plan, the commands, the goals, and the embarrassment. It hit him all at once, and for a moment he just sat there in a stunned daze, unable to contemplate what it could all possibly mean.

About the time Spec was feeling the need for a bit of liquid refreshment, Wing came to his senses and realized that pretty much every muscle, bone, and sinew in his body hurt. He rolled to his side and saw he was still in the garage, and that the crew had moved on, clearly expecting he would have been knocked out for considerably longer. Perhaps he would have been, if they had actually set their weapons to Elephant. But as they hadn't, Wing merely woke with a headache and vision that was wavering and hazy.

And he woke, of course, with a sense of anger that would not be curbed.

It was this sense of anger that gave him the energy he needed to stand up, and to pick up the manual jack by its handle and to swing it around and around until he screamed and let it fly against the wall, creating a crash of metal and glass that resonated through the garage.

That crashing sound went a long way toward making him feel better, even though it scattered those green blobs all over the place, and even though it brought all those little BeeGee bastards back to him, pointing those little rifles again. To hell with them, he thought as he stepped up, fists clenched. Maybe he could pound a couple before they blasted him again.

Someday, maybe he would learn.

The crashing of glass broke his spell. Spec didn't know how he immediately understood what had happened, but he did know he had a rider inside him, a Frangio who had been expecting to call the shots but was now struggling to find its place. And he also knew his buddy Wing well enough to realize he didn't have time to deal with it right now.

When the Frangio had taken root, the wrist and ankle straps of the chair had let loose. Spec took advantage of his freedom to burst through the doorway and elbow a path through the armed mechanics.

"Stop it!" Spec called out. "Don't shoot him! We can help you!"

He wasn't sure if he was yelling, or thinking these, or even both. But he felt the communication touch base instantly.

The BeeGee mechanics halted in place.

No wonder the Frangio could control machines in real time.

Spec stepped between Wing and the line of purple BeeGees.

"You got to stop, too, Wing."

Wing managed to halt his backswing, and found himself standing there in a puddle of flopping green Frangio.

This is when Spec noticed the slimy form of a Frangio slither up over Wing's back and affix itself to the big man's bare neck. Spec nearly choked as he watched Wing's head give an awkward twist to the left.

"Wing!" he cried.

"What do *you* mean, get outta *my* way?" Wing yelled, as if talking to the air. He raised his arm and grabbed a handful of Frangio. "*You* can just get outta *my* way there, buddy-boy." As Wing brought the palm full of goo forward, the creature turned violet, then blue, then all shades of pastel-laced plaid.

Spec felt the entire Frangio essence give a shudder as the slime literally leapt from Wing's hand, fell with a splat, and left a wet trail as it slid away with its gooey tail between its legs. Spec had to laugh when he came to understand exactly what he had just seen. Call it operating system interference, call it obsolescence, call it what you would, but the Frangio had been unable to connect with Wing's brainstem, and his behemoth buddy had repelled the thing's attack—probably without even knowing it was happening.

"What's up, Spec?" Wing said, eyeing the new glow coming from the back of Spec's neck. "If that really is you?"

"Believe me, Wing. It's me. But these are not really the BeeGees."

"Say what?"

"The Frangio are parasites—or, probably more correctly, alpha symbiotes. They've taken over the BeeGees' minds and bodies, and they've been controlling them just like they've been able to control the Bug."

Wing screwed up his brow. Thinking was not his strong suit.

"Seriously, Wing. I've got a Frangio with me now, just like all the BeeGee's do. But it seems us humans don't have the same physiology as the BeeGees. The Frangio can ride along, but they can't take over everything I do."

"What the hell does that mean?"

"It means I know what they're doing. And I know what they want. I think we can find a way to fix all this, but the first thing we need to do is to get those flopping Frangio into another set of tanks."

While Wing and the BeeGees filled a tank and saved the flopping Frangio, Spec held a series of conversations with his symbiote—a Frangio named Lavastar—and a few others.

"Penni lied to us," he told Wing.

The BeeGee blanched to a light pink. "I am sorry."

"It's okay, Penni. I know it's not your fault. The Frangio are the ones controlling everything that's gone on. They don't have any way to move on land, after all, and they can't really build anything. They are deeply intelligent, but completely reliant on their hosts to actually make anything happen. So when they realized Betelgeuse was a short-timer, they decided to take over the BeeGee culture, and use their mobility and craftiness to jump the shark."

Penni shrugged again.

"It turns out that they love racing, though. And when they decided to enter the 500, they found out exactly how much. The feel of the road is intoxicating to them. And adjusting things on the fly, finding the right line ... well, it makes their blood sizzle."

Wing finished dumping the last green Frangio into

its tank.

"I don't understand."

"That Frangio strip we saw those BeeGee crew members remove from the Betelgeuse Bug wasn't alive, Wing. It was a racing casualty. The Frangio misting system failed on the cool-down lap and the Frangio dried out before Xanti Ne could make it back to the pits. It burnt up. Penni told us the Frangio were on an off-day because he didn't want to explain that they were having a funeral."

Wing's complexion suddenly darkened and he bowed his head. If racing teams had one thing in common it was a relationship to death in the inner circle.

"I'm sorry to hear that."

"I've already passed our condolences on to the Frangio contingent. They can all talk to each other all the time. It's pretty amazing."

"Sounds terrible."

Spec smiled.

"Let me cut to the bottom line here."

"That would be good."

"The BeeGees don't want the Frangio in their heads. Both the Frangio and the BeeGees *do* want a safe place to live—and, needless to say, the folks here on Earth are probably not going to accept a bunch of big-assed amoebas riding along in their frontal cortex like they're in some late-night science fiction double feature. To make matters worse, the deal the BeeGees agreed to, heading to Mars, was never really workable because the Frangio need water, and Mars isn't going to have that kind of liquid for a long, long time."

"Sounds like a mess."

"Not really. I've cut a short-term deal with the Frangio."

Penni clapped his hands, then. "Hey! Maari is gone! Maari is gone!"

"Maari?" Wing asked.

"His parasite," Spec said. "They've agreed to withdraw and leave the BeeGees alone to live on Mars in peace when their terraforming expedition arrives."

"So what are the Frangio getting?"

Spec smiled, beaming. "I told them I would show them around the Madison Regatta."

"Boat racing?"

"Of course. It's perfect for them. They love speed, but need water."

"Won't they beat the pants off human boats?"

"Maybe. But maybe not. And if they do, well, maybe they'll get their own circuit. They really don't care about much but water and the physics of going fast."

Penni nodded all his eyes.

"They love going fast," the alien said. "You should have seen them on launch day."

"So what's in it for us humans—or for you and me, for that matter?" Wing asked.

"Think computing power, Wingnut my old friend—the Frangio are living beings, but they're also a great source of computing power, which they'll share in exchange for mobility, for being able to hitch a ride. And we've got something the BeeGees never developed."

"What's that?"

"Robots," Spec replied. "We humans have had robots around the house for so long we take them for granted. And once my Frangio friend learned about all the autonomous technology we humans use, it all clicked."

"Huh," Wing replied, obviously confused. "What clicked?"

"The Frangio link to robots to give them mobility, and in return we get to use their computing power through the same interface."

"Yeah," Wing said, though it was obvious he still wasn't really getting it.

"The BeeGees get free and independent access to Mars, the Frangio's get water and a level of personal freedom that's not been possible before, and we get a huge advance in bio-computing technology that will move our progress up by generations."

"Huh. I guess that makes sense," Wing replied. "Sounds like you've got it all tied up with a shiny little bow, then."

"Yep. We've only got one more problem to fix."

Spec pointed to where the BeeGee crew was standing around the Bug, struggling to keep stiff upper lips.

"Our buddies from Betelgeuse have a driver to support, but that car is clearly not ready to run."

"You're not saying the Frangio want to race

now?"

"No. The Frangio are taking the day off for all the right reasons. But the BeeGees have a certain sense of pride to their craftsmanship, too. And Xanti Ne still wants to race. In fact, he says it's even better that way. More fair."

"They'll never get the pole without the Frangio."

"That's all right," Penni said. "We know we're new at this. But we need to try. And we'll be back next year, too. Mars is in the neighborhood, after all."

Spec looked at Wing. Wing looked at Spec.

Then they all looked at each other.

"Let's get to it," Spec said. "Track's only open for another hour and a half."

Speeding

Many yesterdays ago:

Connor Singh, the man known as the Father of the Chronumentary, switched off his transistor radio and pulled his plastic earpiece away. As always, the lingering, petrochemical-laced smoke stung his eyes, but it was the words of Sid Collins on the Indianapolis Motor Speedway Radio Network radio that brought him to tears. He had listened to them so many times now that he could recite them word-for-word himself:

"We are all speeding toward death at the rate of sixty minutes every hour," the voice of the 500 had said on the IMS Radio Network broadcast. *"The only difference is we don't know how to speed faster and Eddie Sachs did. So since death has a thousand or more doors, Eddie Sachs exits this earth in a race car. Knowing Eddie I assume that's the way he would have wanted it. Byron said 'who the gods love*

die young.' Eddie was 37."

Connor blinked back the tears as he wove his way through a crowd that couldn't bring themselves to leave the scene of the accident, their disbelief and grief a thing of substance, a thing that each absorbed on their own, but that brought them together in that strange way that no one has ever been able to fully explain. The race had already been halted for an hour, and would be delayed another forty-five minutes before A.J. Foyt would eventually conclude the rest of his run that would result in his second Indy 500 victory.

There were 431 highway deaths in the United States that Memorial Day weekend in 1964, but if Connor could pull off this production, the passing of Eddie Sachs would be the one that would resonate across the rivers of time.

Connor considered the radio again. One of the best things about this gig was getting to revel in things like transistor radios. He had bought it new from a trackside vendor just a few hours before. It was gleaming-new, and huge—as big as his hand. It looked futuristic for its time, but also so right—anti-steampunk to steal a later phrase—with its knobs and its dials and its telescopic antenna. He could probably get a fortune for it upstream, but the Bureau was watching him close enough as it was, and pulling relics would cause more problems than he was willing to deal with. With a pragmatic shrug he tossed it into a nearby trash bin, then made his way to the nearly empty area behind the grandstands at the north end of the track where the accident had occurred, thinking about the crash for maybe the thousandth time.

Dave MacDonald started 17th on the grid, but made a mad dash through the field, passing six cars on the first lap. On the second lap, however, he lost control of his red #83 Sears Allstate Special coming out of the 4th turn. The car gave a slow, spinning loop and careened off a concrete retaining wall inside the track, then, trailing orange flame and black smoke that obscured the other drivers' view, shot across the front straight just before the entry to pit lane.

At racing speed, Sachs had only two choices, swerve his gold-trimmed #25 Shrike sponsored by American Red Ball into the path of other drivers, or "shoot the gap" and take the conventional wisdom that tells a driver to aim for that magical spot in the accident where a spinning car should vacate—in other words, charge blindly into the wall of smoke and flame in hopes of finding clear passage. Sachs, ever the professional, chose the latter.

His Shrike speared McDonald's careening car, and it was as if the gates of hell had erupted on the speedway's asphalt. The explosion rocked the crowd of thousands, a second plume of flames bloomed overhead, and the already deathly black cloud became a writhing cloak of poison and corruption and all that is wrong with the world. Neither Sachs nor MacDonald would survive.

It was a helluva sequence.

This was Connor's fifteenth trip to May 30, 1964. This time he thought he had it all, every angle, every sense of dread etched behind the pre-race smiles that rested on drivers' faces. He had captured Sachs himself joking with his team two hours before the race. He had captured young Dave MacDonald practicing feverishly in the weeks prior to the race, trying to tame a car that others said was a rolling death trap. And he had captured the svelte young woman who, the day after, had stolen a solitary moment to scratch an oft-quoted poem on MacDonald's empty pit board.

Connor came to an unused concession stand and scanned the area for any possible witnesses, then slipped his autokey into the deadbolt. The lock opened willingly and he stepped inside, pulling the door closed and re-engaging the deadbolt as the shadowy cool of the concession stand wrapped itself around him.

The storyline he planned was the drama of beloved veteran versus youthful exuberant, but now that he had all the perspectives he needed, something tugged at him.

What's the hook? he thought. *What's going to set this apart? How am I going to come up with something to make this worthy of a "Connor Singh" production?*

The pressure of his success was monstrous. The fact that a fresh batch of Chronal directors were making deals with other physicists just added fuel to the fire. He was the Father of the Chronumentary, but his monopoly wasn't going to last much longer.

Good stories were a yuan a dozen, and hours of fresh footage alone wouldn't do the job. His fans wanted more.

So ... what, then?

Sure, it was an exciting era, and vintage motorsports hadn't seen much coverage yet, but Connor knew his audience. The Sachs-MacDonald story that he loved so dearly would draw interest, but it would wear thin quickly. People forget these kinds of things on a simple time curve.

There had to be some angle, something different.

Something bigger.

He turned his attention to the luminescent face of his period-appropriate watch—or, rather, his wrist piece that looked like a time-appropriate watch. Connor appreciated the irony of the "TIMEX" logo embossed on the instrument's face. Who said physicists had no sense of humor?

In this case, their genius was revealed in what appeared to be a simple wind-up wristwatch, but was actually a TDRP, an acronym for temporal displacement/recall pendant, a device his friend Li-liang Novikoff and he had invented. They pronounced it "T-Drip." The device contained a quantum field reactor and the microscopic temporal control circuitry that would allow Connor to bring his actual temporal transit device (a TTD, of course) back into sync with the current timeline, freeing it from the stasis pocket where it currently resided, out of sight and unreachable by anyone within the current time stream through any other means.

He unfastened the authentic leather strap and removed the faux-Timex, then pulled the stem and held the watch at arm's length. It hovered in the air before him. He tapped gently on the watch's face, and the air shimmered as though someone had tossed a pebble into the atmospheric pond. The Timex winked out of existence, replaced by his temporal transit device which hovered where the watch had been just moments before. An onlooker might have thought the watch had morphed into the data pad, but the two devices had simply swapped places, the watch now residing in a state of time suspension inside the stasis pocket.

Connor paused. His eyes widened and a grin crawled across his face. That was it. That was the hook.

With that, he traced the return pattern on the face of the TTD, then rippled out of existence as the time stream carried him upstream to his own time once again, leaving no trace behind in the empty and silent concession stand.

Many tomorrows from now:

"You're fragging crazy," Li said, shaking his head.

He admired the hell out of his friend, but sometimes he didn't understand Connor Singh's ghoulish passion for chasing dead men through time.

"Yes, it's possible. Of course it's *possible*. We've done the basics a thousand times under controlled conditions, so you *know* it's possible. But what you're proposing is incredibly complex."

"Yeah," Connor replied, flashing his toothiest grin. "And all this other stuff we do is so inherently simple."

Li sighed.

The two of them had worked together for years to perfect and commercialize temporal technologies. Li-liang Novikoff was now known as one of the most brilliant physicists on the face of the earth, responsible for nearly every major breakthrough they had achieved over the course of their efforts. The fact that it was obvious that Li-liang was the better physicist of the two quite obviously pained Connor to no end. But Connor Singh was no mental stiff on his own. He would have made a fine living doing theoretical work if the two of them hadn't met across the ping pong table that fateful afternoon in the university rec room.

Some said Connor Singh, the flashy, enigmatic camera hound, had leveraged Li's brilliance to create a billion dollar industry. But Li understood that it went both ways. Connor pushed him, his enthusiasm and dogged persistence forcing Li-liang out of his overly cautious nature and allowing him to follow his instincts. And Connor was the storyteller, the experiential visionary, the social voice of time shifting. He understood inherently the fact that danger, or at least risk, is the price one pays for changing the world.

Li and Connor had studied Sachs and MacDonald for the past year, each scouring footage Connor brought back, each doing his own semi-investigation of the accident. It was strange, really. What did it say about the two of them that Connor, the daredevil of the duo, had an affinity for the consummately professional Eddie Sachs while Li, the reserved, steady scientist, gravitated toward the flashier youth of Dave MacDonald?

Whatever that oddity meant, one thing was certain:

The two of them together were far greater than the sum of their parts. In fact, it could be argued that the two of them together had completely created every aspect of the world that allowed chronal technology to become what it was today.

"This is the next big breakthrough," Connor said. "And we *are* going to make it happen."

"*Mudilo*," Li said, swearing in his grandfather's native Russian. "You are one ambitious son of a banker. You're going to get yourself killed someday."

"Or perhaps some yesterday," Connor replied with a grin.

"Is this really worth it?" Li asked, knowing his raised eyebrows was his "tell," the tic that Connor would recognize as the sign that Li's own inquisitiveness was piqued and that he was giving in.

"Of course it is. Taking it from the realm of the theoretical to the realm of the practical is what makes it worthwhile. *You* already know *that*."

Li snorted. *"Touché."*

"Let's figure out how to make this work," Connor said.

"You already know there's really nothing to figure out: We just rig up a TDRP to generate a field large enough to contain the transit device and a full-sized adult, then pre-program the TTD to time-jump at the precise moment the TDRP trues up the time streams."

"So," Connor said, "it would dump the pocket payload into whatever time I was in, and auto-sequence me back to our time, correct?"

"Exactly," Li replied. "Time-jump relays have been done before, many times—all that was done as part of the early teleportation experiments, so all of that is very well documented. The hard part will be to program in the proper timing. That will be quite tricky. We'll need to test the whobees out of it."

"Hmph," Connor replied, rolling his eyes. "Feynman and Oppenheimer would be sorely disappointed—we've harnessed time and developed anti-gravity tech, but we can only kinda-sorta do anything even remotely similar to teleportation. We stand on the shoulders of giants, and all we have to show for it is a better point of view."

"Spoken with all the melodrama of a true genius," Li said.

Connor smirked.

"Okay, then. How long is it going to take to put together the mods that will make my 'fragging crazy' scheme a reality?"

Li did calculations in his head.

"Probably a week. Is that quick enough?"

Connor grimaced, but then calmed. "Sooner is

better, but I need some time in simulation anyway. As long as we have the ability to reproduce my exact time transfers, I'd say we have all the time in the world."

Li rolled his eyes in mock disgust.

"To be honest, I'll never understand why you don't just get into temporal archeology. I bet there's big money in that and it's got to be safer than this."

"It's not about the money," Connor snapped at him.

"I'm sorry," Li said, raising his hands in self-defense. This was a sore spot for Connor, and one that had been on critics' lips for the past few years. "I do get it. I'm sorry. I know you've always preferred to be where the action is."

"It's all right," Connor said, rubbing his eyes and remembering the sting of oily smoke. "I'm sorry to snap. It's just that I'm so tired."

Li also knew it was something else, too. Something Connor would never admit to. Being in the middle of several hundred thousand people grieving like that took its toll on a man, even a happy-go-lucky theoretical physicist who was doubling as a theatrical wizard.

"All right, then," Li said. "I'll conjure up the quantum wizardry required to make this happen—in the meantime, don't you have a story to edit?"

"Yeah," Connor said. "It would be good to get it far enough together that I just drop in the new stuff."

"And be ready to go straight to distribution."

Connor gave him a strange glance.

"What," Li said. "You think I haven't learned a little about the entertainment business from you?"

Connor smiled and half-bowed to Li in a theatrical show of respect. "You're a quick study, Li-Liang Novikoff—and a damned good friend."

"Okay, then," Li said, "let's get to it!"

Li went over the equipment and the checklist one last time, then scanned the transfer code before putting his bio-stamp on it. Then he handed it to Connor to perform the required counter-verification. Connor re-executed the fine calibration on the temporal transit device as he did before every trip, taking extra care this time as he worked through the lines of code that would initiate the auto-sequenced time jump that would re-designate him as the primary payload. Li appreciated the fact that Connor was taking this seriously. Even though the testing had been flawless, the exercise scared him.

Satisfied the device would home in on his trace, Connor applied his bio-signature to commit the programming, then handed the device back to Li.

"Looks like we're ready," Li said.

The two shook hands per their long-established routine, then embraced each other before parting with firm pats on the backs.

"Godspeed, traveler," Li said in a well-practiced tone.

"God *particle*, engineer," Connor completed their ritual with a flourish.

With nods and smiles, they finalized the handshake, then parted. Connor stepped onto the temporal platform.

"Be careful," Li said.

"Don't worry, Mom," Connor said, "I won't be later for dinner."

Li pressed the initiation icon and the platform shimmered. Connor rippled out of existence, leaving Li feeling a bit more lonely than usual as the chill rush of air that accompanied a transit swept over him.

Many yesterdays ago:

Connor sat on the starting grid behind the wheel of the number 25 car, his fingers tapping impatiently on the wheel. Thanks to the wonder of the Personal Holographic Image Projection technology he had borrowed from the Hollywood makeup crews, he was completely indistinguishable from Eddie Sachs, right down to the lemon on a string that Sachs wore around his neck to provide much-needed liquid refreshment between pit stops.

He had successfully abducted Sachs earlier in the morning by posing as a crew member, which enabled him to catch Sachs alone in the garage area for long enough to administer a fast-acting sedative and to stow him in the stasis pocket.

Connor fought back anticipation—he "knew" Sachs's number 25 car like the back of his now-gloved hand because he had put in countless hours in the holosimulator, driving this very track in this very car, in an environment as indistinguishable from this time's reality as he was now from the real Eddie Sachs himself.

Tony Hulman's voice came over the public address system.

Gentlemen, start your engines!

Connor's adrenaline immediately shot through the roof.

He took a deep breath and flipped the ignition switch, then braced himself for noise and fury as his crew brought the engine to life. The engine thrummed with deep power, beating out a familiar tempo. The holosimulator had admirably reproduced this actual experience, including the engine's vibrations and the smells around him. But this was something special. This was real. Complete. The audience would eat it up.

All thirty-three cars on the grid roared to a start, then the crew members rushed for the pits as Connor and the other drivers in the field pulled away for the parade laps.

The pack rumbled around the Speedway for two laps before the pace car peeled off to release the thundering herd.

His nerves were ragged. Even though Connor knew how it would end, and even though he had made this run hundreds of times in the holosimulator, the anticipation gnawed at him. What if he made a mistake? What if he drifted too far on a corner? What if he missed something? Knowing the microscopic camera built into his goggles was recording his every move increased his anxiety. He wanted this to be perfect, and now that he was here he knew Li's concern was well-placed. He didn't want to have to come back for a re-take.

He maintained position through the first lap exactly as Sachs had, holding his line and driving hard, dreading that moment when Dave MacDonald would inevitably spin as they exited Turn 4. He focused on settling into his race rhythm, pushing aside doubt by drawing on the knowledge that the pre-programmed T-Drip and TTD would safely pluck him from the cockpit at just the precise moment. Connor drove on, confident he would be transported back to his own time, no muss, no fuss, and complete with the necessary holovid footage of the drive right up to just microseconds before the moment of impact.

The audience would eat it up.

All he had to do was follow the damned script.

The field crossed the start/finish line at the end of Lap 1, and a peaceful calm came over him as he started on the brief-yet-fateful journey toward Eddie Sachs's date with destiny.

Coming out of North Chute and into Turn 4 for the second time, Connor sensed more than saw MacDonald's slide to the inside wall, out of control, but he clearly saw the flaming red car careen back onto the track in front of him. He braced himself instinctively as he felt the shimmer of the time transfer begin: The familiar coolness wrapped itself around him and reality shifted, rippled, then refocused again, revealing ... MacDonald's flaming car still directly in front of him.

The last thought that went through Connor's mind before impact was, *"Something's wrong,"* and, then, nothing.

Many tomorrows from now:

Li stood over the inert but still-breathing form on the departure platform. After all the research they had done on this project, Li would know this man anywhere.

It was Eddie Sachs. Not Connor disguised as Sachs using PHIP technology, but the real, genuine Eddie Sachs, thankfully still unconscious.

Li looked over the driver's sleeping form, dressed out in his white racing suit, his long face slack with slumber, his short hair receding, and he wondered where the hell Connor Singh was. He went back to the chronal control screens and accessed the memory playback functions of the temporal transit device.

What had happened?

Why wasn't this *Connor?*

He accessed the event replay, and a note popped up.

Li,

If you're reading this, I hope I'm there reading it along with you. If I'm not, then you should be able to find the holovid footage stored in memory. I added a fail-safe in the code in case something went wrong, a hidden routine that automatically downloaded the holovid footage from my camera to the T-Drip, just in case. So, even if I'm not there, you should have the final footage. Go ahead and finish off the edits. I'll leave it to you to figure out what to do about the narration. I'm sure you'll figure something out. I know you already understand distribution (grinning).

If I'm not there, make sure you capitalize on the 'Connor Singh, lost in time' angle to help promote the film. If we're going to make history while recording history, we might as well benefit from it all, eh?

C.

Li turned from the screen, his eyes misting.

Damn Connor Singh.

He pounded the table.

Why did Connor do that? What did he think he was doing, writing code? This is why his friend was not a world-class physicist. This was why he had to run to the arts. He had no discipline, no patience for this kind of work.

Tears pooled in the corners of his eyes.

Damn Connor Singh.

In the end, though, Li understood exactly why his friend had done it.

The thing Li admired most about Connor was that he could spend hours working to get the exact right timing on an audiovisual sequence, and when he was done, it would be perfect. They would come out of those long, grinding sessions that Li himself found tedious to a fault, and Connor would be glowing, gushing with excitement.

He was a natural-born storyteller.

But for some reason Connor couldn't accept the idea that deep physics was not his thing. He wanted it all. He wanted to write the code and understand chronal currents and mass transfer effects and drive cutting-edge investigations into the dark-matter studies that were racing along at what, for scientists, was a breakneck pace. And he wanted to tell stories and take images and race through time. He wanted it all.

But like the separation between the world's greatest race car drivers and those who are just competent, Connor Singh was not a world-class physicist.

It was simple as that.

Connor Singh made a mistake, and he paid for it with his life. Li took a moment to confirm what he already knew in his heart.

It was the fail-safe download of the holovid footage that screwed everything up—without being properly validated, the programming interpreted the download as the target re-acquisition swap, the step that would have put Sachs back in the cockpit of his Shrike, and deposited Connor back into the time pocket. Thanks to Connor's surreptitious code addition, once the holovid download was complete, the auto-jump occurred, dumping the payload of that time pocket back to the acquisition platform—which, in this case happened to be Eddie Sachs himself.

Sachs stirred. The sedative was wearing off.

"Whaaaat thhh ... " The driver rubbed the back of his head and looked at Li through bleary eyes. "Feels like Parnelli done whupped me upside the head."

Li froze, unprepared for how to deal with a time-displaced traveler.

Sachs shook his head and crab-walked away from Li.

"Who the hell are you?" Sachs said, his eyes wide as saucers.

"I'm Li-liang Novikoff," Li said.

He stepped behind the desk to put something between himself and Sachs. He was afraid of this man. Sachs didn't belong here. He was a wild animal in ways, a man from a rugged time when men solved problems with their fists and drove race cars wrapped in a hundred gallons of flammable fuel. Li felt like he was suddenly caged. He thought about the hallways behind him where he could bolt and shut the doors.

"You a Commie?" Sachs asked with raised eyebrows.

Li shook his head. "Buddhist."

"Aren't they the same damned thing?"

"No. Not really."

"Fair enough," Sachs said, relaxing noticeably as he slumped against the wall and let out a rumbling sigh. He looked around, puzzled by his surroundings. "Mind telling me where I am?"

Li looked at the man and saw that behind the bravado, he too was scared.

"You're with a friend, Mr. Sachs," he said, coming around the table to help the Clown Prince of auto racing to his feet, "and I think we have a lot of talking to do."

It was impossible to explain the complexities of time travel to Eddie Sachs, but he got the basics right away.

"It's like that book," he said.

"What book?" Li replied.

"That time machine book by the cat that done the Mars thing on the radio back a long time ago."

"Yes," Li said. "But it was H.G. Wells that wrote the stories, and Orson Wells that did the radio play."

Sachs shrugged. "Hoop-te-do."

Once Li settled down a notch, he found Eddie Sachs to be an easy-going man with, naturally, a great sense of humor. He was also a quick learner. Li explained the project, and he showed Sachs much of the work Connor had already completed.

"I don't get it," Sachs said. "Why focus on Davey and me? I mean, why not Parnelli, or Jimmy, or AJ? They's just as gooda drivers and got just as gooda chance of winning."

Li gazed at Eddie Sachs, not certain how to proceed.

But Sachs got the gist all by himself.

"We die, don't we? Me an' Davey?"

Li merely swallowed and nodded.

"Makes sense," Sachs said, sitting back with pain on his face. "Folks always focus on the accidents."

They were silent for a moment.

"Can I see it?"

"I don't think that's a good idea."

Sachs looked up at him with his face steeled. "I'm a racer. Let me see what happens."

Li didn't know what the right thing to do was, but in the end he believed that a man has a right to see his own fate. He called up the segments Connor had already created, and he let them run.

Dark lines etched themselves on Eddie Sachs' face as he watched the red #83 get backwards and ram sideways into the barrier. Blood drained from his face at the sounds of squealing tires, the sight of the fireball erupting. The crushing rumble of the explosion. Voices came through time, voices no other historian had been able to capture.

Li turned the machine off, and let Eddie Sachs alone to digest the moment.

"Your friend's in that car now?"

Li nodded.

"You gotta send me back."

"I don't know if I can do that," Li said, though the truth was that he had been thinking about how he might be able to do just that. "I can't send a man to his grave."

"You sent your friend."

"But he wasn't supposed to die."

"I know. I was. So just send me back and

everything will be right again."

"I don't think I can do that if I know you're going to die."

"And you think I can let another man die in my place?"

Li stared at Eddie Sachs and saw a streak of honor in the man that burned deeply.

"Send me back earlier, and I'll switch places with your friend."

Li shook his head. How could he explain all the nuances of this to Eddie Sachs, a man from the 1960s who by his own admission wasn't even that mechanically minded anyway?

"The physics don't allow for two TDRPs to be in the same past together. The best I can do is to possibly put you back into your original time stream just as Connor was supposed to transfer out."

"I see," Sachs said. "That would be just as the accident is happening."

"So you see why I say that if I send you back I'm sending you to die."

"I don't know about that. Maybe I won't."

"What do you mean?"

"Haven't you heard," he said with one of his patented Eddie Sachs smiles. "I'm the greatest driver in the world. I know what's right ahead of me this time. Maybe I can save it."

Li thought about it.

Maybe he could. The reaction time was nearly nil, but nearly wasn't zero. Maybe the greatest driver in the world could do it. Maybe. And if he did, what would happen then? How would the world change? Would he and Connor even exist? It was enough to make his head hurt. He thought about Connor, burning to death in the inferno on the front stretch of Indy. He looked at Eddie Sachs. What would the fragging *mudilo* do here?

"All right," he finally said. "I'll set it up."

Sachs scratched his chin and looked at the freeze-frame image of black smoke obscuring the track.

"You think I could get some chocolate ice cream before I go?" he said.

Li smiled.

"Yes, I think that would be good. Perhaps for both of us."

Li-liang removed the code Connor had added, of course. And he tracked the stream that the footage Connor had captured came in on to ensure he had the proper moment selected for the next swap. He gave Sachs a TTD unit, coded to interact with the TDRP that was still on the wrist of Connor Singh back on May 30, 1964.

He shook hands with Sachs before starting the event.

"Godspeed, Eddie Sachs," he said.

"Got that damned right," Sachs replied with a grin that was half tooth, half chin.

Sachs stood on the platform. Li toggled the process. The platform shimmered and rippled and Eddie Sachs disappeared.

All that was left was the waiting.

Things went well, though.

Connor Singh appeared on the platform, and Li yelled at him and bitched to him about never doing anything so stupid again. And Connor got that sheepish laugh about him that he always got, then changed the subject by talking about footage and editing and image adjustment techniques.

It took Li the rest of the day to decompress, but decompress he did. He checked on the historical registers to see that, no, Eddie Sachs had not altered history, that he and Dave MacDonald had still perished together. It tugged at Li that he had been the last person to see Eddie Sachs alive. The thought made him feel like a failed guardian angel. But it was all right, all was as it should be, and that was the important part. His spirits lifted when he checked in on Conner and saw that, yes, he was still going a billion miles a minute on the project, so all was indeed as it should be. He had a long afternoon of cleanup to do on closing the jump process, and he threw himself into it with enough vigor to make the hours pass in the blink of an eye.

Later, though, in the few quiet moments before he closed up shop for the night, Li thought about his life. He thought about what they were doing with time. He thought about the running joke among temporal physicists' about being able to do anything since the TDRP/TTD combination gave them all the time in the world to work in.

That was wrong, though.

We are all speeding toward death at sixty minutes an hour, Sid Collins had said. And no matter what timelines we occupy at any moment, a person has only a scant number of heartbeats, only one life. Minutes spent in the past may well give us their lessons, and minutes to be lived in the future offer their hope. But it is the minutes of the present that matter.

Li-liang looked at the photo of Dave MacDonald that sat on his holoscreen, he remembered the images of flame and smoke that had filled so much of his life the past year, and he saw an image of himself and Connor Singh in their early twenties that he had called up on his personal data system. They were staring off to the side of that picture, Connor pointing to something as if it must be something important. It was so long ago.

Yes, he thought. It's only the moment at hand that we can actually do something with.

And he vowed to never forget that ever again.

Oh-oh

My name is Joneem A'lonn. I'm an undercover agent for the Vice Division on D'Garzi, which happens to be the fifth planet in a system the humans know as HR 8832, which seems like kind of a stupid name to me, but that's not what I want to talk about today. What I want to tell you about was the time it was my job to stop the Edaligo crooks who were planning to steal billions of universals by fixing the most-wagered-upon event in the established universe.

Indianapolis, Indiana. May 30, 1969. My cover name was Johnny Malone. I ran a hot dog stand stationed smack dab in the middle of the fourth turn Snake Pit.

Despite the fact that it was barely ten o'clock, it was already plenty hot. Today's race would be a tough one. Of more immediate concern, however, was the sunburned male and female humans who stared at the menu behind me with glassy eyes, both obviously having imbibed more than their daily recommended requirement of Southern Comfort. I could almost hear their brain cells screaming as they expired.

"Gimme two dogs with relish and catsup. Hold the mustard," the male said.

"You got it," I said back.

I reached into the steamer and grabbed two hot dogs. "That'll be sixty cents. The condiments are at the end of the counter."

The male gave a skewed grin.

The female blushed and snarfed into the back of her hand. "Far out," she said. "I didn't know they made 'em in mint."

The male leaned in close enough that I could smell the sour mash and Pepsi. "That's groovy, man. But, uh, she's got her period, so I don't think I need a condiment."

"Bummer," I said, pointing. "The catsup and relish ... are at the end of the counter."

While the two went to squirt catsup and dole out relish, I got a better look at the female. She was an attractive sample of the human species—tall and thin, with straight yellow hair held back with a wilted daisy chain. She wore a tie-dyed tank top knotted at the shoulders. The garment covered an ample pair of mammary glands. To each their own, I suppose, but humans like mammary glands in a way I'm sure I'll never understand. Take, for example, my love of the meaty hot dogs that I'm peddling right now. They're great—absolutely fantab-u-lous. But I don't wander around with signs telling people to show me their wieners.

I shook my head in wonder as the pair staggered away, hoping my behavior was humanlike enough. I must have done fine, because the people kept coming and the dogs kept flowing. Of course, it could just be that I was in the middle of the Snake Pit, and it wouldn't have mattered if I was a green-tentacled Zanabian.

I pressed the blue button on the atomic scanner and looked out over the grandstand as often as I could.

No sign of Edaligo activity ... yet. But it was early, and we had a tip that something was up. The data said that each of the last three years a driver named Mario Andretti broke down or crashed or, in some unbelievable event, managed to somehow not win the Indy 500. He even lost a wheel after starting on the pole two years ago. Lady luck, the humans said. Rigged game, the D'Garzi Gambling Commission cried.

Not that the humans knew any of this, of course. Their ignorance is an important element of the game because it creates the sense of fair play and integrity that our bookies stake their reputations on. This was Earth, the most entertaining place in the Milky Way, vacation place of the stars, home of the hundred fine arts, hot dogs, and—of course—the exalted Frisbee. Nothing so ugly as game fixing could be allowed to pollute this cash flow.

It was personal to me, too. Despite the rumors, I put twenty-five thousand universals on Andretti. Call me a sucker or just call me your run of the mill D'Garzi—we're all gambling fools—but Mario is my favorite and I couldn't imagine coming to the Brickyard and not laying at least a year's pay on the line.

I know—a little extravagant. Let's talk about your problems.

The morning progressed, the Purdue Band played, and the golden girl danced. Sam Hanks kept announcing little tidbits about the upcoming race, and the folks in the Snake Pit kept drinking and dancing and waving their signs. Eventually, the pit crews rolled the cars out into the famous three-across formation. I had just finished serving a foot-long Coney dog when I pushed the blue button again.

There. On the track.

Son-of-a-clack.

I couldn't make out a specific form, but the atomic analyzer gave a low-frequency streak that indicated the presence of Edaligo brain function on the racetrack, somewhere around the first turn— right at the front of the grid.

Gotcha.

I pressed the red button, and everything around me came to a stop. Nothing changed for the humans, of course, the temporal displacement merely put me in a timestream that moved much more rapidly than theirs.

I checked all the gazes quickly to ensure no one was looking directly at me. Everything seemed far out and groovy and all that, as they say for about everything here.

The blonde female and her old man were heading my way again; the phase shifter had caught them in midstumble. I needed a diversion, and those ties at her tank top gave me the perfect opportunity. I walked over and pulled the strings, leaving her ample mammaries exposed. This would most certainly be enough to attract a crowd, and that would help cover the disappearance of me and my hot dog cart.

I hit the button again, and the temporal displacement shut down. The woman shrieked. Not a soul noticed my dinky hot dog stand wink out of existence.

This is why humans will never be part of the Universal League, by the way. Too easily distracted. Hell, the Wentashian Congress alone can take as much as a quarter million years to prepare a simple colonization mission. Can you imagine the problems a flighty species like humans would create if they were thrown into the universal mix?

Still, they have Walt Disney, so they can't be all bad.

The Edaligo come from Tau Ceti's third rock.

They are tall, lean, and more than a little on the nasty side, especially when they're awake. To be blunt, the Edaligo are a damned ugly species in about every way imaginable. They smell like the Dark One, they take advantage of early intelligent life if you let them, and they ship their nuclear waste into deep space rather than deal with it themselves. They had one of the more active interstellar syndicates in the universe, and though they hadn't stuck their noses into anything big for quite a while, that only meant they were up to something big.

To make matters worse for us Vice guys, the Edaligo are shape shifters with unlimited scale, meaning they can go big as well as small.

Have I mentioned that I hate the bastards?

I made my way toward the grid. The cars were all lined up, the drivers seated.

"Gentlemen, start your engines."

The throaty roar of thirty-three engines came across the field, and I couldn't help but get all goose-pimply thinking about the front row of A. J. Foyt, Mario, and Bobby Unser.

I glanced at the atomic wave scanner but it was blank. The Edaligo was playing it cagey, now.

Where would he hide?

By the time I made the pit entrance, the cars were rolling away amid a cloud of dust and the sweet smell of exhaust. I searched the crews and found nothing. I scanned the home stretch grandstand. I headed toward the tower and the pylon. Nothing.

The parade and the pace lap finished up. The cars barreled into the straight, and the green flag waved. Cars roared into the turn, Mario ahead of Foyt and

Unser. What a thrill. What a thrill. Did I tell you I love my job?

Come on, Mario, I thought, rooting for my favorite as I turned my attention to the Edaligo.

Bruce Walkup was the day's first casualty, dropping out of the race halfway through the first lap due to transmission failure. On the second lap, Billy Vukovich's Mongoose threw a rod. Art Pollard lost a driveline on lap eight, and Ronnie Bucknum burned a piston on seventeen. Jim McElreath's engine burst into flames in lap 25. George Follmer's went two laps later. By the time Gary Bettenhausen lost a cylinder on lap 35, I knew something was up.

I made my way up pit lane. The teams would be pitting soon, and all the guys in the funny fire suits were lining up with their tires and their fuel hoses.

Foyt and Roger McCluskey had both slipped past Mario, and Wally Dallenbach and Lloyd Ruby had joined with that trio to make it a five-car race. But McCluskey ran out of fuel, and while he coasted around, the other cars flooded into the pits under their own power. A.J.'s crew won the day's first pit battle, and Foyt screamed away a little under fifteen seconds ahead of Mario.

I scanned each team as they worked. Nothing. The track, I thought, with a chill. The Edaligo could actually become part of the track if they wanted, choosing just the wrong moment to transform into an unforeseen oil slick. I looked at the tower. That was the only place I could get a clean scan of the entire two-and-a-half-mile circuit. I sighed. I don't like to use the temporal shifter too often because it can attract attention, and attention is one thing D'Garzi Vice doesn't need.

But this was important, so I hit the button and slipped through the crowd to climb up into the tower. Still, I found no sign of the Edaligo anywhere. Strange, I thought, scratching my head and turning to head back downstairs.

My foot caught something small and hard.

I lost my balance and fell to the floor in a jumble. The atomic scanner clattered down the first three steps and burst into a jillion pieces.

"Dammit!" I said as I rubbed my elbow.

A tiny voice came from behind me. "Oh-oh. So sorry."

I whirled.

It was a creature no more than a meter tall, carrying a gnarled wooden walking stick that, once you untangled all the loops and twists, was certainly bigger than the creature itself. It stared at me with a sense of the wondrous in its shiny black eyes and its gray-skinned expression. Its clothes were tattered and frayed, made of a material as rugged as burlap.

"What the hell?" I said. "Are you some obnoxious lawn ornament, or what?"

The thing jumped onto my chest with a force impossible for its size.

"Wait a minute," I said, struggling vainly to get out from under this thing. "The temporal displacement unit isn't supposed to work on more than a single creature at a time. You shouldn't even be here."

The thing raised an open palm and gave an offhand shrug. "Oh-oh," it said.

The atomic scanner burst into flames from the third stair. Enough was enough. I struggled toward the burning scanner, but couldn't budge an inch with the weight of this thing on my chest. Without that unit I would never find the Edaligo.

"Get yer feet off my person before I remove them for you!"

"Hehehehehe," the thing said, then whacked me upside the head with his gnarled stick.

"Ouch!" I saw stars. "Hey, take it easy, sport. Nobody has to get hurt here, especially me."

The thing squeaked as it giggled and waved the stick above my nose again. "Leave my feetsies alone!"

"Yeah, uh ... groovy. All right?"

It gave a cheesy grin.

I inched my hand toward the disrupter I had clipped to the back of my belt. A second later, I whipped the weapon out and squeezed off a shot that would blow the thing to Delta Pavonis.

The mechanism clicked.

Nothing happened.

"Oh-oh," the lawn ornament said with another shrug. "Lemme see that." He tried to snatch it, but this time I was too quick for him.

I scrutinized him closely. "What are you doing here?"

He pursed his lips and whistled a little too

nonchalantly, drawing one heavy toe across my chest. "Oh, nothing." But he glanced over at the scorer's table nonetheless, and my internal warning sirens went off like a Betelgeuse klaxon.

"You were going to mess with the lap recorders, weren't you?"

The lawn ornament's eyes got wide, and he gave a brown-toothed smile. "Oh-oh!"

I was growing to hate those two syllables.

"Gimme," the thing said, motioning the disrupter with his cane.

"Let me up and I'll let you play with the disrupter." I realized it was a mistake as soon as I said it, but the words were out of my mouth, and besides, I quite honestly didn't think I would ever make it back to the standing position any other way.

"Deal!"

I tossed the disrupter a short distance away, and the little guy leapt off my chest. I took a deep breath, feeling like an Arcturan constrictor had just let go of me.

"What the heck are you?" I said, standing and dusting myself off.

The creature pushed the disrupter's trigger. Every person in the room was suddenly wearing polka dots of assorted colors.

"Hehehehehehehehe!" He pushed the button again and a life-size portrait of Tony Hulman went up in flames. "I like it!" the thing nearly cried with glee. "I really like it!"

I wracked my data structure, trying to figure out

what this creature might be. Finally, it all started to connect. Cars dropping like flies, the scanner breaking into flames, the disrupter doing ... whatever the heck it was doing.

"You must be a gremlin!"

"Coodle-doodle-doo!" the lawn ornament replied, did a backflip, and pointed the disrupter at me.

I dived out of the line of fire, and a potted plant behind me melted into a liquid pool of something that resembled chicken soup.

"Holy Frembock!" I said, somehow managing to rip the device away from the creature.

It screamed and tried to jump for it, but I held the unit over its head, and it jumped and jumped until it was obvious that approach wasn't getting anywhere. "Leprechaun giver!" it screamed. "Double-crosser!" It whacked me across the shins with its stick.

"Ouch! Damn it, that smarts!" I hopped on one leg, but still managed to keep the weapon out of the thing's lightning-quick hands. "Don't do that again or you'll never see another disrupter as long as you live."

The thing gave an expression of profound sadness.

"You are a gremlin, aren't you?" I replied.

It cowered, and its eyes flicked from corner to corner. "I'll be damned," I said. "An honest-to-goodness gremlin."

Earth's airmen once referred to gremlins as causing persistent trouble with their planes. Earthfolk have blamed these gremlins for all sorts of machine and device failures since then, but D'Garzi scholars had assumed they were just making these guys up. Humans have never been able to design for flop, after all, and a pack of "gremlins" are a convenient crutch to fall back on during performance review time.

"That would explain the problem with the temporal shifter, too," I said.

The gremlin gave an exaggerated, toothy grin. "Oh-oh?"

I looked at the atomic scanner that lay shattered and scorched on the stairs. I looked at the gremlin. Then back at the scanner again. There was no way the scanner was going to work, and therefore no way I could locate the Edaligo.

"Gimme back my thingie!" the gremlin said, trying to whack me on the shin. "We had a deal."

"I didn't say how long you could keep it."

The gremlin rubbed the hairy wart on his chin. "You got me there okey-dokey."

"But I'll make you another deal," I said, thinking as quickly as I could. I pulled out a standard contract. "This time it will be a little more binding."

"What do you got?" it said, eyeing the disrupter greedily.

"What's your name?" I asked.

"I am—" It puffed its chest out and raised a fist triumphantly. "—Fred-a-rico!"

"Well, Fredarico, here's the deal."

A few minutes later it was official, this time signed and sealed and binding in all settled colonies of the

Universal League.

I clicked off the temporal phase shifter as we shuffled down the stairs. Above us, the control tower erupted in a roar of confusion as their clothes suddenly sprouted polka dots.

We started at turn 1 and went toward turn 2, then the backstretch and turns 3 and 4. Not surprisingly, nothing much happened except that Fredarico left behind a trail of broken grills and fried transistor radios.

I realized then that none of this was really Fredarico's fault at all. The little guy loved gadgets and gizmos, but they didn't love him. Beyond that, I was willing to bet that my scan would have proven what I was already guessing—that gremlins' skin bends light, making them nearly invisible to the human eye. "Oh-oh," Fredarico would say, and a cursing drunk would shake his radio or press his earpiece deeper into his ear.

I started to feel sorry for him.

I mean, that kind of a reception has got to be wearing on a little guy after a while.

Still, I hadn't found the Edaligo, and the race was wearing on. We hit the pits just as the leader and crowd favorite Lloyd Ruby was pulled into his pit stall, right in front of us.

"Hop to it, Fredarico," I said, pointing.

Perhaps I forgot to mention this, but, you see, the Edaligo evolved their shape-shifting capability through generations of what human science fiction writers are calling nanotechnology, or bugs. They write enzymatic programs that define a specific shape, and the machines take care of the rest. But even the Edaligo's magical technology didn't stand a chance against Fredarico.

The gremlin jumped over to Ruby's car.

A high-pitched scream came from the rear cowling. The revving engine covered up most of the normal spectrum, but my subsonic aural detector read the unmistakable sound of the Edaligo death scream loud and clear. Fredrico gave one of those openhanded shrugs, and I didn't have to be a lip reader to know what he was saying.

Jackpot, baby.

A puddle of fluid dripped onto the asphalt under Ruby's car, and his engine revs dropped a notch. I realized the Edaligo had morphed into the fuel pump and had been feeding Ruby's car a little extra oomph. Suddenly it all made sense. Ruby wasn't a long enough shot to raise eyebrows when he won, but he wasn't a bettor's favorite, either. My guess was that a quick check of the records would show a significant amount of Edaligo universals had been wagered on Ruby.

"Come on back," I said to Fredarico, waving him over to me.

He jumped off the cowling and used the fuel line as a stepping point. A second later he was back over the wall, and Ruby was tearing out of his pit. The sickening sound of burning rubber and ripping metal screeched out.

"Oh-oh," I heard Fredarico say.

I couldn't help but laugh. Ruby's crew had forgotten to remove the fuel hose, and connected end had ripped a massive gash into the side of the car. A river of fuel sluiced over the concrete. Ruby's day was done.

Fredarico and I kicked back and watched the rest of the race together. To make a long story short, Mario Andretti won his first Indy 500.

Per our contract, Fredarico acquired the Edaligo spacecraft as salvage. This turned out to be a first-contact mission after all, and the appearance of such an interesting new species warranted investigation. What better way than to send them to a place where technology ran everything?

Hehehehehehehe, as Fredarico says. Serves the Edaligo bastards right.

Me?

Well, I got a big raise. Nothing pleases a commissioner who's up for reelection like scamming an entire crime syndicate. So now I'm a captain. And I learned something important—Fredarico loved Mario. He had been planning on hopping a ride in Andretti's Brawner/Hawk after he messed with the scoring guys. So just between you and me, I wasn't surprised when Mario didn't do so well in future races. I suppose I could be wrong about the little guy, but all I can say is that I never got that singsong "oh-oh" out of my head, and that alone was enough to keep me betting on Unsers from that point on.

I can also report that my wager paid back at two-to-one. Not a bad gig if you can get it. So with my spare cash and the extra two weeks of vacation I got with the promotion, I could think of only one thing to do.

You got it—I went to Disneyland.

Ghost of a Chance

Though she wanted desperately to be the last human being alive, the remnant core of Chandra Kumari—those parts of her that had not yet deg'ed, anyway—knew she was not.

Billions of cross-linked spectators from across the galaxies rode along as the almost-human part of Chandra Kumari sat gripping her olde-tyme steering wheel in her out-of-date AI construct and guided her simulated Granatelli STP Turbine Special (complete with its remarkable gas turbine power plant that had been derived from a helicopter engine and its advanced four-wheel drive technology) out of Turn 3 and into the short chute.

The #14 of Foyt's car filled her mirrors as Chandra rolled the turbine toward turn four. It was a caution period. Their pace was now languid enough that her processor spun with unbidden information: *A. J. Foyt. Four time winner. Car owner. Photos with broad grins and dark scowls. Hats with odd brims. Milk. A moving clip of a stout man in a racing helmet pounding the back of his automobile with a hand wrench.*

Foyt had been a legend. A real racer.

When Chandra looked at the oil-stained nose of the Coyote racer, the part of her that was still human cycled with a deep sense of pathos that was, to her, so vitally important.

The idea of racing against Foyt made her feel so … unworthy.

"My race, my terms," she said to herself, gripping the wheel. *My race, my terms.* It had been true so far. The event had unveiled just as her schedule had called for it to.

She had maintained the lead even with a pace slightly below historical. She had sacrificed a few restarts to reduce stress on the STP Special's drivetrain, relying on the car's ability to maintain its blistering pace to overtake the slower competition.

It had been frustrating to see competitors run away, but so satisfying to chase them down again and leave them behind. It felt too much like the old stories of a tortoise and a hare for her tastes.

It had worked, though. So far, anyway.

And if it worked here, it could work again.

For the cycles it took the turbine to roll a mere five feet as measured by the humans of the period, Chandra's processor considered what her co-riders would think of her master plan.

They had no idea where she really was, after all.

Her co-riders had no idea that, unlike her

competitors (whose race environments were made of the more standard software interfaces, doped cross-chronal Einstein chips, and hacked-up feeler code), her system was a physical cockpit with real steering, real pedals, and a set of motion mechs positioned to mimic g-forces, the turbine's power delivery system, and every other tactile sensation the situation demanded. They did not know her visuals were presented on a sleek, spherical display that encased the cockpit like a pod. And they most *definitely* did not know that this rig, when combined with her First Gen construct, gave her something more—the chance to practice what it would be like to pilot an actual vehicle.

To actually *drive*. Yes, that was the word. *Drive*.

It let Chandra Kumari *drive* an automobile like a real human being.

And, finally, these spectators had no idea that back-tracing the relativistic space-time transformations being made to place her actions into context at the Computation Control Center (CCC) would put her on a small Terran Alliance transport cruiser named *Godspeed*, or that this same transport was, at this very moment, boring though the quantum foam of sub-space toward olde Earth itself.

All they knew was that Chandra Kumari, the overall points leader of the current Tru-Code Historical IndyCar Series and a two-time Indianapolis 500 winner, was guiding her DayGlo red turbine racer through the short chute at the end of a yellow-flag caution period, that she was leading the race, and that this was fateful lap 197—the lap that had spelled doom for the real turbine and Parnelli Jones (its original human pilot). The turbine wasn't the fastest car at the Indianapolis Motor Speedway in Standard History Year 1967 AD, but until a notorious $6 gear-box bearing had failed on fateful lap 197 it had been able to maintain a pace close to its 166 MPH qualifying speed—something none of its competitors could do.

Some of the observers currently connected directly to Chandra's cross-dimensional stem were there because they wanted to recall that sense of being that had once come so naturally, that same sense of *humanness* that Chandra longed for. These "fans," mostly other original uploaders who retained enough of their core essences, shuddered with anticipation as Chandra rolled her right foot over the accelerator. They enjoyed feeling the ruddering thrum of power and hearing the whine of turbine blades as they spun up.

But they were not the only observers of this greatest spectacle in automobile racing.

Gambling comes naturally to cultures formed on streams of data, and for every explorer who tied into Chandra's race stream to get a blast of their human past, several more came to revel in the probabilistic scrub of odds against random chance.

Each of the cars' Probability of Failure (PF) algorithms were calculated from known failure rates and modified by knowledge of manufacturing methods of the period. The turbine was unique—

just as every other car had been. Each part had its own idiosyncrasy, each its own behavior, and therefore, each its own PF.

And now, trillions of Uni-creds were flowing across book lines.

Because, as fate would have it, no sim pilot in the history of Tru-Code racing had ever managed to get farther than Parnelli Jones had.

None.

So the co-riders gambled.

As the laps ticked by, the wagering grew more and more frenzied.

Would the car break down? Or rather, since no turbine-powered car had ever survived, the more popular bet was: Which part would break this time? Transmission? Clutch? Gear box?

A fiery crash?

None of those questions mattered to Chandra Kumari right now.

She shunted her processor so she could focus.

At the beginning of the race, she had bought into the idea that she was trying only to cheat fate, that she wanted nothing more than to bring her turbine-powered machine home with 200 laps under her belt.

But now Chandra wanted to win.

She could feel it in her registers.

She could taste it in the accelerometer-lined pressure nodes that covered her "fingers," the gripping systems that connected her to the steering wheel and sent signals that spurred up in metallic vortexes of current and rushed through her thought processes. Excitement came in flashes and flares that tasted sharp and vital across metallic traces.

She loved these moments.

She needed them.

Chandra had once comm'ed with another racer about these feelings of anticipation that grew inside her as the last laps of a race unwound, about the crystalline clarity of now-ness that competition brought to her comparison routines. She told this racer that her processor loops got tighter in these clicks, and when that happened, her focus routine dropped into netherspace. She was surprised when that other racer had exchanged nothing beyond a sense of bewilderment.

It had been as though she was speaking to a system that was unable to parse her.

Embarrassed, she had stepped away from that interaction.

But she could not deny her own emotions. Chandra Kumari was, at her core, a race car driver. And right now Chandra Kumari was a race car driver who wanted very badly to win.

She kept her eye on the flag stand as she led the field onto the main stretch.

The green flag was unfurled.

Where Gurney's naturally aspirated Eagle or Foyt's Coyote Special would respond with an immediate throaty roar and a burst of acceleration, the turbine grew to its speed like the wail of a solar flare, thin at first, but growing steadily to a wild scream. Wanting to give her power plant enough time to gather acceleration so she wouldn't get caught-out by her challengers, Chandra rolled onto the throttle early with *ever so much* more pressure, smoothly, calmly, hoping to avoid tearing something up with the turbine's torque.

The mid-mounted turbine power plant to her left spooled up with a soft whoosh, a sound quiet enough she could hear the gears engage as she up-shifted.

The sensation of speed pressed against her construct's "back."

An ache grew where her raising heartbeat should be.

Then the green flag was waving, and Chandra's STP Special hunkered back as it accelerated towards the yard of bricks that marked the start/finish line.

This would tell the tale.

G-forces raked her through Turn 1.

The turbine whooshed again as she steered through Turn 2 and let the car drift up to the wall and run down the back stretch.

Billions of virtual spectators leapt to their feet. If Chandra and the turbine could make it down the back stretch and into Turn 3, there was a real chance that a galaxy full of longshot bets would pay off in spectacular manner. The only odds that mattered to Chandra, though, were the PFs mapped to her vehicle.

Would they catch up to her as they had the others?

She felt the edge of anticipation in her human pieces.

The need to gamble is predicated on a need for risk and for fear, built on the ideas of possibilities and anticipation. It was no surprise that the biggest sim draws replicated periods when speed was high and technology was growing. The perception of danger was what brought observers to things like race simulations in the first place.

The start/finish line flashed by, signaling the start of lap 198.

She had done it—taken the STP Turbine farther than any other construct.

It wasn't enough, though. It had never been enough.

The Turbine Special chewed up another two-point-five miles of virtual asphalt, and lap 198 was complete. Her lead over Foyt's fading #14 was seven seconds.

Another circuit and it was eight.

With one lap to go Chandra eased off the throttle to limit stress on the drivetrain. She should have no trouble as long as the car stayed together.

Cheers echoed across the entirety of the Terran Alliance as she passed the start/finish line for the final time.

She let the turbine wind down as she coasted on her victory lap, waving to spectators who greeted her with a standing ovation.

She had won.

That piece inside her coded structures felt

"good."

Or at least she knew they were supposed to feel good. But she was growing ancient, and with each upgrade Chandra Kumari had grown less and less capable of hiding the fact that more of her humanity had deg'ed out. It was to the point that she wasn't sure which parts of her were human and which parts were not.

Now, trying to bask in the satisfaction of what should have been a glorious victory, Chandra wondered if the sensations she felt were real, or if they were just echoes ringing in hollow space. Was she actually happy, or was she merely pretending she was happy because that's how she knew she should feel? Was the fact that she was aware of her missing parts causing her to pretend those parts were really there?

These fears bothered her.

They were why she was on a transport heading to Olde Earth to begin with.

Not that anyone would know that.

Yet.

After wheeling the car into Victory Lane, she allowed herself a moment of quiet to let her circuits settle around her.

The real test was coming. Soon.

She clocked her system down and cleared her registers.

Then Chandra opened the channel for the virtual interviews.

* * *

Perhaps the most surprising thing about the singularity was that it was not self-inflicted.

For the few originals—the survivors—the pieces of code and command language that came straight from the first uploads, survival was a both boon and a burden.

Every newly formatted human since that time was created with complete access to all public data sets, and full knowledge of their history.

Here are some facts they acquired:

They learned that immediately upon mastering sub-space travel, ancient humans began searching for new life—new worlds that could be directly inhabited or terraformed to meet human needs. During those first explorations humans encountered other species, though none as technologically advanced as themselves. On the whole, humanity gave many of these new species great gifts and provided for advancement. When a species was deemed unsuitable for upfit, they were placed under review and provided protection.

They understood that the Terran Alliance took shape over many standard millennia, and had at one time included several new species.

Then probes revealed the Tetraxenons—a new species that was unlike all others.

At first they were mistaken for simple, glob-like masses of organic material that were somehow able to exist in the cold vacuum of deep space. But the Tetraxenons were soon found to be capable of travelling through sub-space dimensions at will, and, after considerable investigation, Alliance scientists determined these masses were actually biological constructs created by the Tetraxenons. The aliens traveled through the dimensions within these bio-constructs like Jonah traveled in the belly of the whale—except, in this case, the Tetraxenons were chemically linked to their "whales" and controlled them the way a captain commands his crew.

The bio masses were literally the Tetraxenon's space craft.

More analysis revealed the Tetraxenons' lack of any form of mechanical or mathematical computing, as well as their total absence of metallurgy, manufacturing technology, and deep physics. They were not carpenters or builders of complex structures. They were, apparently, not deeply philosophical or religious. Everything about the Tetraxenons and their biological constructs was chemical in nature, and purely organic—all grown through random processes rather than "made" or "manufactured." There were no computer circuits to analyze, no parts or pieces to reverse-engineer, no labels, no printouts, no languages or communication devices to read from, no way to understand anything at all about the Tetraxenons and their civilization except to become one with their chemical existence.

On the counter side, human technology appeared to be just as alien to the Tetraxenons.

As such, communication was not an option.

What was clear, however, was that the Tetraxenons soon came to view humanity's movement into their space as humans might view a virus entering the body of a child: a plain and simple threat that had to be eradicated.

Hence began the first inter-galactic conflict of aggression.

Fortunately, the Terran Alliance still remembered its roots, and despite their peaceful intent, all Alliance vessels were well-armed.

Unfortunately, the first altercations between the Terran Alliance and Tetraxenons were still a bloody shock to humanity and all its allies.

Fortunately, the Terran Alliance managed to survive, despite great loss.

Unfortunately, the Tetraxenons recovered human remains after the initial battles, and their analysis allowed them to bring new and different weapons to bear during subsequent skirmishes.

After months of apparent calm, the Tetraxenons launched simultaneous attacks on all forty-five planets of the Terran Alliance.

Tetraxenon masses dropped into orbits around each planet, and employed spore-based systems. Within days it became obvious they had reverse-engineered the human genome and designed a horrifically effective bio-weapon. More than 95% of the human race across the entirety of the universe was dead within what the CCC would later estimate to be a standard week. Other species did not fare as well.

Some survivors remained in space-based platforms or aboard ships in transit. Those survivors, though, could literally never go home.

And the Tetraxenons continued to hunt them.

Total extinction was merely a matter of time.

Humanity responded by downloading themselves into lifeboats made of symbiotic AI hosts, systems that, until then, had been used only for the elderly and disabled, and systems that were immune to the Tetraxenon weapon. This move allowed minds to be saved. And once those minds had been fully placed into code, duplication programs allowed for their rapid replication. Where human *bodies* became extinct in the blink of an eye, the use of symbiotic AI hosts allowed for human *thought* to grow at a rate limited only by their ability to create hosts.

And hosts, it turns out, were a snap.

Before the Tetraxenons could adjust their approach, unmanned Terran Alliance transports emerged from sub-space *within* the Tetraxenons' home planets and created the unstable, planet-consuming plasma bursts that are known to occur when sub-space quantum noise comes into contact with large quantities of physical material like the molten core of such a planet. The subsequent explosions were, of course, catastrophic, and spewed material and high energy gamma detritus across the universe that can still be studied to this day.

Humanity's executors were thus executed, and humanity lived on.

After a fashion.

The host AI wrappers, the base platform upon which the core of thought and expression existed, were refined and improved. Intelligence grew at remarkable rates as information was shared at rates that had previously been impossible.

But the core, the digital representations of human traits—a sense of wonder, the ability to feel, to think, and to love … they suffered the centuries-slow degradation that is common to digital storage, boiling away into netherspace in fragments of binary flares—a process that had become known as "degging," or having "deg'ed."

First Generation Terrans, the truest children of humanity, felt it the hardest.

They reported feeling lost and listless at times.

Empty.

They were going to live forever, but they described the sensation of degging as being aware they were leaving pieces of themselves behind like detritus scattered across the centuries.

It was like, Chandra Kumari once said, becoming a living ghost.

Nearly fifty minutes later, Chandra set a flag indicating she would take one last question.

A reporter from the Wide Universe of Sports Network logged a query and was acknowledged by Li Mei, Chandra's publicist and manager. She had anticipated this—both the reporter and the network were supporters of the series and her team.

"Thanks, Chandra—this is Veril Drox of WUSN. We span the cosmos to bring you the *human* drama of athletic competition. Congratulations on the victory. How would you say your performance measures up on the scale of *human* drama?"

Chandra hesitated.

Despite her preparations, she still felt skittish.

She recovered her composure, checked with Li Mei to see if it was truly acceptable to release the news, and (after receiving the "go" flag) replied.

"Good question, Veril, and one I often ponder myself."

She hesitated.

"As you know, since the beginning of the Virtual IndyCar League, I and my fellow competitors have relied on full system linkage to provide your viewers the complete experience of what it was like for a human being to drive an automobile at speed. These links connect us to the simulated automobile, and flow directly to our riders, providing ocular, auditory, and tactile connectivity."

"Of course," Veril said. "As WUSN viewers will recall, you let me sit in your place during practice earlier this year, and it resulted in a remarkable collection of bent metal!"

"Indeed it did," Chandra replied, hoping her sarcasm wasn't overly obvious. "But I can now report two new things about today's race."

"New things? Do I sense a scoop?"

Chandra paused just long enough that she knew

Li Mei would be happy.

"Well, I'll leave it up to you to decide for yourself."

"Fabulous! Shoot away."

"You see, Veril, today, instead of the normal net connections and CCC translations between me, my riders, and the sim, I chose instead to utilize an old-style pod, complete with manual controls and a spherical audio/visual display that required me to observe the environment with my own optic and audial receivers—my own "eyes and ears" as they were—and translate that information into responses that I input directly into the simulation using pure olde-tyme human interfaces."

It was an entire picosecond before Veril replied.

"You mean you were using actual brakes and throttles and …"

"Exactly."

"Steering?"

"Yes."

"Gear shifts?"

"All manual."

"You can't be serious. I can't believe you were able to use olde-tyme controls and still get the STP turbine to make it around the Brickyard 200 times."

"Well, Parnelli Jones managed 197 laps, which is better than any hard-wired performer has ever been able to accomplish. I think that alone says my IndyCar performance did a better job of faithfully replicating the *human* drama of sport than any other experience, don't you?"

"Couldn't have said it better myself," Veril replied. "And I would say the massive registers of followers who have just jacked into the replay would agree."

"But it gets better."

"Better than that?"

"You'll remember I said I have *two* pieces of news."

"Play it on us!" Veril said with a tacky tone to his com-stream.

"Another thing your riders don't know is that at this very moment I'm on an Allegiance transport that is in mid-transition to an exit point plotted to take us to the lowest orbit of Olde Terra itself."

"Earth?"

"Exactly. The place at the root of all humanity. Once there, I'll be undertaking the challenge of completing a true 500 mile race while piloting a fully physical replica of this same 1967 STP Turbine Special."

The connection filled with a metaphorical gasp.

Another picosecond passed. Then another.

Finally.

"You mean?"

"That's right, Veril. The Lightspeed racing team has secretly been working to refurbish the old Brickyard, complete with its traditional yard of bricks at the start/finish line. They've also been able to find engineering plans for cars of that era—specifically including Andy Granatelli's beautiful turbine automobiles. Everything is in place now. I can't wait to arrive."

"I am globberstopped."

"I hope you're less globberstopped when the contract between Lightspeed and Wide Universe of Sports Network gets signed, which should be about ..." Chandra waited a moment, and got Li Mei's concurrence. "Now."

"This is fantastic!"

Veril's tone changed to full promo mode, speaking to the rest of the universe rather than to Chandra herself.

"You've just heard the scoop of a lifetime, friends. Terra itself! Olde Earth! The birthplace of the Terran Empire and the graveyard of humanity. Grande Champion Chandra Kumari and Team Lightspeed are taking us all back there, back to experience true *human* achievement firsthand through the miracle of the virtual omnipresence entertainment network."

"About that," Chandra said.

"Yes?"

"I want everyone to know this will be a true human experience."

"What do you mean?"

"I think I'll leave this last twist to my publicist to announce," she said. "But let it be known that my entire goal in all of this is to have the most human experience it's possible for me to have."

"And, by reference, then," Veril said, sensing the conversation was at its end, "allow our followers the same."

"That's right, Veril."

"Sounds completely remarkable. Thank you for the interview, Chandra. And, once again, congratulations on your victory!"

"Thank you, and thanks to your viewers for tuning in to the 196th Annual Virtual Indianapolis 500, presented by the Tru-Code IndyCar Series and the Wide Universe of Sports Network."

With that, Chandra cut off her com-link, disconnected from the session, and closed her eyes to compose herself.

Only a few cycles later, a query alert came from her publicist/manager.

On the whole, Chandra liked Li Mei. He didn't try to sugarcoat things or win her over like other celebrity-pleasing sycophants did, nor did he treat her like a pampered idiot. They both knew they needed each other, and they respected the strengths of each other's base coding. This created a relationship that bordered on friendship and allowed them to be, when warranted, as frank as necessary with each other.

Right now, however, she was still trying to get her processing settled back into the proper ranges of norm after being so focused on the race and then the pressure of the interviews. The lack of stability to her situation made her testy.

"Yes, Li Mei," Chandra said. "What do you want?"

"I just wanted to personally congratulate you on your victory, and the great interview," Li Mei replied.

"Is there anything I can do to help you prepare for the upcoming exhibition?"

"So we're calling it an exhibition, now?"

"The term 'media circus' seemed too bold, darling," Li Mei replied.

Chandra gave a chuckle and settled down.

"Dear, sweet Li Mei," she said. "Call it an exhibition if you will, but we both know you didn't just call to congratulate me—credits deposited in my accounts are more than enough for that. So what is it you need?"

"Honestly, Chandra! Your suspicions harm me!" Li Mei paused. "I merely wanted to see if there was anything I could do to help you with the next stage of preparations ... or, perhaps, see whether there's any way you might change your mind about one or two little things."

So that was it.

Li Mei wanted to discuss her decision to run the race wearing her First Generational host construct. It was an antique system, actually ambulatory. It had two working "legs" and robotic arms. It was encased in a form of "skin," with molecule-thin strain gauges and other attenuators that allowed the unit to show expressions on its face. The unit Chandra was going to use was, in fact, the very system that had served as the initial life support prosthetic for the original, *human* Chandra Kumari, the woman who had first downloaded to AI symbiote.

"We just tested it," Chandra said. "It will be fine. I'm actually still riding in it now."

"There are better choices," Li Mei said.

"You mean *safer* choices, right?"

"You could upload yourself to a hardened extra-vehicular construct designed to survive harsh planet conditions, or one designed for heavy lifting and extreme force ... just in case the worst happens. Or you could use an omnipresence net construct and pilot the vehicle remotely, which would be just as thrilling for your audience."

"I'm not doing this for the audience."

"I know," Li Mei said with resignation, "Your race, your terms."

When he had first heard her pitch for this project, Li Mei had immediately grabbed onto the marketing elements of it, just as Chandra had expected he would. But while Li Mei was busy developing spin about *celebrations of human achievement* and *reclaiming the birthplace of humanity*, for *laying the groundwork for re-terraforming Earth to make it fully inhabitable again*, Chandra had been working on her own plan. Her only goal was to experience life as a human being.

And that meant she had to deal with life and death.

True risk.

"We've been through this before," she said. "I want to know what it's like to be truly human again. Loading into my First Gen construct, and actually driving is the closest I'll ever get."

Li Mei clicked disapproval. "That construct was designed to enable you to participate physically in a world full of true human beings. Its full-body construct made them comfortable around you, but it offers no more protection than a human body would offer."

"That's the whole idea," Chandra replied. "No chance of damage, no risk. No risk, no adventure." *No adventure, no life,* she thought to herself. "What good is achievement if victory is merely a matter of iteration over time?" Chandra continued. "What good is victory if it's pre-ordained by our ability to throw infinite copies at a problem?"

"You're taking it too far, aren't you?" Li Mei asked.

"No. I'm not."

"At least let us take a safety image of your core before you leave?"

"You know better than to ask. Human racers had no safety core."

"Yes, I know. And human race drivers died, too. Don't you think they would have taken safety images if they had the chance?"

"We've discussed this enough. Removing the *human* element would negate the whole thing."

"Now you're sounding like a Primativeer," Li Mei said, invoking one of the small clusters that continually argued that the Alliance should create a fully replicated primitive lifestyle of a type found on olde-tyme Earth.

"Don't be like that," Chandra said.

"How did they say ... ?" Li Mei replied. "If the boot fits?"

"All you care about is keeping the money rolling

in."

"Of course I do, dearie. I fully admit the boot fits both ways."

Chandra moved her construct to the porthole in her compartment and gazed out at the mesmerizing patterns of the *Godspeed*'s flight path through subspace.

"We can't study human nature by removing risk," she said. "We're already doing as much as we can to ensure my safety, and this last simulation shows I can maintain margins. The dangers are acceptable."

The hesitation before Li Mei replied was greater than transmission called for.

"Do you recall the old human saying, Chandra? The Jews can never return to Jerusalem?"

"What does that have to do with anything?"

"Do know what it *meant*?"

"Of course—it was a colloquialism some used to describe the loss of the Israeli state after the third nuclear obliteration."

"Yes," Li Mei said, "but the more *human* perspective behind that colloquialism is that the Jewish people were fundamentally changed when Israel ceased to exist. In effect, it said there *were* no Jews to return to Jerusalem, just as there was no Jerusalem to return to."

"Now *you're* beginning to sound like an Enlightenist."

"Touché."

"If you're trying to say there are no humans because Earth was scorched, you're wrong. But I say that *if* there are no humans it's because the Tetraxenons destroyed us, and *if* there are no humans it's because after migrating to this form, we've actually changed—deg'ed out so far that we've lost track of who we are. The existence or non-existence of the home planet is not relevant."

"And yet," Li Mei replied, "we carry on as echoes of our creators."

"What are you trying to say?" Chandra replied.

"Attempting to honor our progenitors by replicating their weaknesses rather than utilizing the abilities they imbued us with seems to be inherently disrespectful of their memory."

"I think you're wrong," Chandra said. "I think that as long as we carry enough of our humanity to recall it, we are *still* human. And I think we are being disrespectful of our human memory only when we *ignore* that part of us that comes from them."

"Tell yourself whatever it takes, Pancake," Li Mei replied with a flourish, clearly unwilling to press the issue further.

Chandra chafed—she hated it when he called her "Pancake," a nickname that stuck during her early racing career thanks to her tendency to push too hard on oval courses, which inevitably ended with her car "pancaked" against the wall.

"You're not going to convince me to drop my plans," she said. "I'll run some more probability scenarios if that will make you happier, but in the meantime I suggest you spend your time stirring the propaganda machine to ensure we get the cash flow you love so much."

"Oh, don't worry about that, dearie. Advance sales alone will fund this trip *and* your next season."

"Assuming I don't retire."

"You shut your com-ports and be still my algos!" Li Mei replied. "Are you *trying* to give me a gray-out? If you retire, I might have to get a *real* job!"

Chandra chuckled. The very idea of Li Mei working was funny.

"Enough crazy talk," she said. "We'll chat in three weeks."

Chandra dropped her link, and scanned sub-space again.

"My race, my terms," she said to herself. "Just as it's always been."

At what point do you become so far removed that the term "life form" no longer applies?

Godspeed's primary navigation and guidance element, congenially known as Godspeed Primary Pilot One, initiated the command to bring the ship out of sub-space. Though imbued with many human decision-making traits, the pilot class was created devoid of the full range of emotions that would make up a fully sentient personality. There was, however, enough innate curiosity and inquisitiveness there to temper its otherwise dispassionate decision-making abilities, thereby making for a successful autonomous "pilot" algorithm. These traits gave Godspeed Primary Pilot One its semblance of consciousness.

The passenger onboard this trip piqued that curiosity.

Godspeed Primary Pilot One was aware of the passenger's identity and of the overall nature of the trip. News feeds indicated Chandra Kumari was a First-Generational Terran Citizen and that she was planning to complete a 500-mile run at the newly reconstructed Indianapolis Motor Speedway.

Using a standard-issue First-Generational construct.

This seemed remarkably unreasonable.

Or stupid.

Yes, that was the term.

This idea seemed stupid.

First Gen constructs were brittle and required the actual core of the citizen to sit inside it.

Their slower reaction times to auditory and visual cues would mean more likelihood of error. The reduced motive power behind their synthorganic musculature, and the lack of sheer strength of their outer coverings made them less durable.

Misfortune while in such a construct could lead to eternal shut-down.

The First-Generational construct was so inferior that Godspeed Primary Pilot One could calculate no possible reason why one would use such a form to complete such a dangerous piloting exhibition.

It was an unnecessary risk.

Calculated risk—and the ability to engage in such activities—was a significant portion of the algorithm that made Godspeed Primary Pilot One successful. It was, therefore, perfectly logical that Godspeed Primary Pilot One would place a speculative wager on the results of the exhibition with forty-six-to-one odds of potential failure should First-Generational Terran Citizen Chandra Kumari choose to go through with the exhibition using a First-Generational construct.

Godspeed Primary Pilot One's pair-mate side processor, Godspeed Primary Pilot Two, had performed its own calculations on the probability of First-Generational Terran Citizen Chandra Kumari *actually deciding to use* a First-Generational construct for the exhibition, and Godspeed Primary Pilot Two had then placed its wager (with more conservative odds) on the outcome that First-Generational Terran Citizen Chandra Kumari would decide to back out of the original framework, and opt to use a more appropriate—and more durable—Planetary Environment Excursion construct to perform the exhibition.

Although Godspeed Primary Pilot One was incapable of anything as complex as a sense of humor, it found Godspeed Primary Pilot Two's wager to be ludicrous. Had it been capable of understanding the concept, it would have categorized the wager as "laughable." Any good pilot understood the risk-taking aspect of First-Generational Terran Citizen Chandra Kumari well enough to understand that her choice had been made specifically *because* it carried both the greatest possible reward and the most possible danger.

This discrepancy between Godspeed Primary Pilot One and Godspeed Primary Pilot Two was due to its creators' use of pair-mate algorithms to make life-or-death decisions. As long as a process didn't run into a stalemate of endless loops, pair-mates balanced risk and reward better than unique individuals—which explained why Godspeed Primary Pilot Two was not provided self-awareness beyond making such input into the decision process.

Godspeed Primary Pilot One was aware of self-awareness, though based on its own brief calculations it suspected this self-awareness was probably over-rated. That line of processing, however, was nowhere near as rewarding as the risk/benefit analysis that went along with wagering. At a programming level so deep it was not fully conscious of it, Godspeed Primary Pilot One was quite happy it had been imbued with such elaborate predictive calculation capabilities.

As such, after making its wager on Chandra Kumari's event, Primary Pilot One turned its attentions to the Frontier Crop Production Probability tables—harvest time was approaching on several frontier planets, and it found potential biological algorithms more interesting than sports-related algorithms.

Once *Godspeed*'s sub-space transition had completed and there were orbital mechanics to deal with, Godspeed Primary Pilot One engaged its pair-mate interface with Godspeed Primary Pilot Two.

Together, they set the craft on a path to atmospheric entry.

Systems are rarely perfect the first time. Or the second.

Chandra stood on the asphalt surface, dressed in her flame retardant suit and carrying her open-chinned helmet. Her race goggles hung from her neck.

She "breathed in" the aromas of fresh grass and motor oil that came on the breeze.

The timing was perfect.

Given the position of the sun, it would have been something called Memorial Day. It was late morning, but the temperature against her thermistors was "pleasant."

There was none of the ceremony that had accompanied the actual event. Jim Nabors did not sing "Back Home Again in Indiana." The Golden Girl did not lead the Band of Purdue. But Chandra still felt the power of the moment as a warm place in her code.

By the time she arrived at the track the news was fully out.

Everyone knew her core had been flashed into her own First Gen host, and that for all purposes she was now what an olde-tyme human would call a robot, a self-contained entity that functioned as a totally separate individual.

The design documents and project summaries left behind said the human and the AI symbiote had actually merged in these systems—that human personality, emotions, and thought patterns combined with AI and a complex collection of manufacturing and electrical engineering to create a seamless human/AI symbiosis.

It wasn't quite like that, though.

Chandra's system *did* work together, but if she worked at it she could still sense gaps between the pieces.

Perhaps those gaps were because of who she was. As a First-Generational Citizen, Chandra was so sensitive she could theoretically still isolate those pieces of ideology, experience, and sensation that came from her initial download. Perhaps she was just too advanced to merge as completely as the handbooks suggested she should.

She doubted it, though.

Regardless, Chandra could still feel everything. Her modern-day calculations tumbled unfettered through her processors, just as before. She felt the usual friction between the gating functions of her thousands of sub-systems as they worked with involuntary precision to keep her core operational. She noted how the construct's interfaces dragged down her processing power to match a humans', a state that seemed drudgingly slow at times and achingly glorious at others. Chandra could almost feel electrons race down her arms as the limb eventually raised or fell.

The anticipation was marvelous.

But, as she stood on the track, what Chandra Kumari focused on most was the vast sense of distance that suddenly existed between her and her actions. What she found herself thinking about was how remarkable the simple act of movement was.

That movement, when performed in Terran Alliance's ship, had been intellectually satisfying. But here, standing on the seemingly limitless surface of Olde Earth, the idea of movement made her systems want to crash.

She was alone—the only sentient being on the planet.

And she could *walk*.

She could *move* without interface to any other being. She could *run*. She could do … *cartwheels* … the word snapped into her head for the first time that she could ever remember. *Cartwheels.*

Except for the fact that she no longer could recall what one was, Chandra could have done a *cartwheel* right here.

It made her smile. The lips of her construct bent upward.

She felt "good."

Her DayGlo red Andy Granatelli STP Turbine Special sat on the starting grid at the outside of the second row—6th fastest on qualifying day—along with the thirty-two other replicas of open-wheel cars that comprised the field.

She went to the vehicle and ran a hand over its wide racing tires. They were slick and black. They smelled of strangeness.

She strolled down the track, her systems clogging as she took in the brightly painted automobiles.

There were names painted on each. Real people's names. *Gordon Johncock. Jackie Stewart. Jerry Grant. Jimmy Clark. Unser, Andretti, and, yes, Foyt.* She knew them all. She could feel them. Standing here before this race, she could feel the presence of these drivers, and it made her utterly aware of how small and how trivial she really was.

Nothing could make her human again.

Nothing could make her a real race driver.

Not like these drivers were, anyway.

Not like them.

For a moment, she wanted to call it all off, but then she got to the last row, and turned to look forward. A fresh flare of challenge hit her. It wouldn't do for her to be at the back of the field. She strode her construct forward, and by the time she arrived back at her turbine, her race face was on. She ran her hand over the STP Special's chrome roll bar one more time.

The cars had been prepared in precise detail.

Nothing had been strengthened. Nothing re-engineered.

They were as solid—and as weak—as the originals in every way.

There would be no PF algorithms in play today.

Actual tire wear, fuel use, and metal fatigue would rule the day for Chandra and her turbine-powered race car, as well as the rest of the cars competing against her.

Correction: *Taking part in an exhibition* with her.

She grinned at that, too.

Her favorite headline in this morning's feeds had been: *Yes, But Can She Make 200 Laps In a Real Car?*

The wagering taking place now certainly treated the race as a full-fledged competition, and that's how Chandra was approaching it. As she did in the simulation, she wanted to beat Parnelli Jones, the best human driver of the time. She planned to drive the hell out of her car today, planned to drive it better than Jones had.

She was going to glory in the feeling of actually *driving* every inch of these 500 miles. She would feel g-forces on a nine-degree bank, feel heat and fatigue, sense pressure from other drivers.

She wanted to feel truly alive for the first time since upload.

She wanted to belong.

But, just like in the sim, Chandra knew she wanted to see that checkered flag, too.

Chandra Kumari wanted to win.

So she was going to do exactly what she had done in the Virtual 500. She would protect the machine where she could, and let it run in others. The car was capable of going the full 500 miles *and* winning, so that's exactly what she intended to make it do.

Chandra put on her helmet, slipped into the cockpit and buckled her harness. She pulled her goggles up, tightened the chin strap, and waited. A moment of silence later, she remembered to connect the hard-wired links that would carry her data stream back to the rest of the universe. As soon as the link authenticated itself, the infamous call came to her coms.

Start your engines!

Her hands tensed on the steering wheel as her virtual pit crew got to business. The turbine fired as planned, spooling up and sending smooth, thrumming vibrations through the chassis. All around her came the raking snarl of internal combustion engines. The vibration of sound was intense. Smells of exhaust were oddly sweet. Chandra was disappointed she couldn't feel a shiver crawling up her spine, but there was only so much the First Gen Construct could do.

The flag controller dropped a signal, and the field began to roll.

She fell immediately into the deep concentration that came so naturally to her, that sense of professionalism that served to hone the moment to a sharp newness as she shook her STP Special out. She scanned the needles—temps, pressures, and fuel light. She ran up the gears, and back down, feeling the way her legs moved through the chassis, fighting the physical pushback of the clutch and the brake.

It was beautiful, similar to the simulation, but different in ways she couldn't begin to put into words.

She rolled the steering wheel to bring heat into the tires.

Her "shoulder" pushed against the side of the cockpit as the car twisted back and forth.

Brilliant.

The parade laps ticked off too quickly for her

liking.

And, before she knew it, the field was running at full throttle, the green flag waved, and the race was on.

Where there is no script, there is no certainty.

Chandra drove with precision.

The road came as a rushing stream, and the sound of the air scrubbing her helmet was a soundtrack that helped focus her mind.

The discrepancy between her quantum co-processors and the construct's reactions gave her time to absorb things around her as she raced. It was as if she were two different people, one driving and another sitting behind her and watching her shift and steer, and checking her mirrors, and experiencing motion with limited politeness at her rivals as they blocked her.

The draft of other cars pulled her along.

The whine of tires on asphalt was like no sound known to history. The simulations had gotten that wrong, giving it a high-pitched whine rather than the firm throb of reality. The sounds of engines buzzed around her, and time seemed not to exist.

She was driving.

Really driving.

It was the most beautiful sensation Chandra had ever felt.

At lap 100—the halfway point—Chandra had a momentary image of herself from outside her construct as if the second part of her were a literal ghost sitting on the roll bar as she turned steady laps. Her second raised its "arms" and screamed out loud as fresh air streamed through her. She felt the hard wall inches from her tub, and watched the snake-like dance of the white line painted inside the corners as they slipped under her front tires.

That core that still saw herself as human registered the idea of this vision as a daydream, a hallucination, something that perhaps defined the very essence of what it meant to be human.

Lap 150 came and went, with Chandra maintaining a comfortable lead while cruising just below the stress limits she had calculated of the car's potentially problematic drivetrain.

Lap 160 saw her still in the lead, as did laps 170, 180, and 190.

Lap 197 approached with no yellow flag in sight.

Some things had not changed, though, and true to form the AI-powered A.J. Foyt doppelganger was still in dogged pursuit in spite of trailing her by almost twelve seconds.

Chandra maintained her pace.

Through lap 197.

Through lap 198.

As she crossed the yard of bricks to begin lap 199, Chandra Kumari was so close to victory she could "smell" it. *Two more laps,* she thought as she raced down the front straight, lifting to get into the corner. *Two more laps,* as she guided the DayGlo car down into the banking.

Two more laps.

The disaster occurred as she eased off the accelerator.

A hairline fracture on a compressor vane, the car's second-most fragile piece, went terminal then, shredding itself, shearing its way through the engine to pulverize the rest of the blades. A whirling cyclone of supersonic shrapnel tore through the machine, igniting the gasoline that powered it.

The Paxton turbine engine exploded with a thunderous blast.

A wall of fire and black smoke blanketed the first turn. The car disintegrated into thousands of parts, and what remained of the DayGlo chassis careened wildly up the track on a direct path toward the concrete wall, Chandra Kumari still strapped to her racing seat.

Chandra's processors cut time into discreet moments.

A bit of steel whirled before her eyes. A rear wheel flew away with the slow-motion force of the explosion. A river of flame flowed over her construct's plastic skin until that skin became a liquid stickiness that then turned black and evaporated into smoky vapor.

The wall was a white strip against the cobbled asphalt.

The sound of impact was sharp, deep, and blunt.

The world spun.

Cycles later the wreckage of the STP Turbine

Special came to a screeching halt, bits of rubber and metal still burning, the fuel cell belching a deathly black cloud into the blue May sky.

Race control commanded the other cars come to a halt, and a silence hung over the great superspeedway. In geosynchronous orbit above the now-still Indianapolis Motor Speedway, Godspeed Primary Pilot One and Godspeed Primary Pilot Two both initiated recovery protocols.

Equipment that had been used to rebuild the speedway rumbled back into action.

If ghosts were not real, would it be necessary to create them?

The piece of Chandra Kumari that was still human knew before the first shard struck that her chances of survival were dim. As she sat in her tub of broken steel with fire building around her and smoke billowing in intense sheets, she tried to move an arm and then a leg. Shrapnel had cut all connections, though, and nothing happened.

She tried to speak to the network, but her vocal routines were gibberish.

Her processor flickered in ragged bursts of static.

She was alone. Truly alone, as indeed were all human beings in the end, before upload.

Machines came to her side, equipped with cutters and firefighting equipment. They sprayed dust that colored the smoke, but the flames were too intense.

They're too late, she thought. *Is this what it's like to die?*

An image went through her core, then.

She had been a little girl, sitting on a fence in an open field. The breeze was filled with daffodils and the fresh scent that comes in spring when the trees are growing their leaves. She raised her arms in a sign of victory, and felt the wind blowing freely in her hair as she fell off the perch to land harshly on the ground below.

Then it was gone and there was only fire and smoke and the machines that were still following their algorithms to complete their attempts to save her.

As her processor began its final shutdown processing, Chandra's optical sensor glanced back down the track one last time, back to the yard of bricks that marked the famous start/finish line.

She saw images.

Human forms.

Were they her imagination? Remnants of some distant programming? A resident blur of electron decay on processor space? Were they a piece of code running in her still human basis? A sub-routine called at the last moment?

Or were these specters? Spirits? Ghosts?

Whatever their source, they continued to come forward. Rows upon rows, standing at the yard of brick.

Chandra Kumari knew them well.

Vukovich. Bettenhausen. Unser. Sachs, Ward— drivers, real human drivers standing in their race suits, wearing helmets and gloves, their faces smeared with the grit that comes from living a life on the edge.

The fire burned around her.

The emergency crews worked.

And around the universe, wagers were laid both for and against the long odds that Chandra Kumari would survive.

It's okay, she thought. *I'll be okay.*

And here at the Indianapolis Motor Speedway, one by one, these specters of racers who came before her who either were or were not merely inside Chandra Kumari's mind, opened their arms to welcome her back to where she belonged.

Do Android Drivers Dream of Electronic Flags?

WEEK 1: PRACTICE, PRACTICE, PRACTICE

The low *whoosh* of the hydrogen-fusion power plant reverberated off Indy's grandstands as the Aoku-Alpha Special sped down the main straight toward T1. It was a practice run, early in the month. Trey Hannigan felt the chassis thrum and the engine reverberate as he applied pressure to the right control stick and eased the vehicle into the turn. The sensor in his inner ear tingled as the suspension compressed in response to g-forces.

This wasn't his grandpa's kind of automobile. It was essentially a disk-shaped airplane that was smashed down into the space between four tires.

Every element of the car was connected to him in

some fashion. The revs indicator lit cones along the side of his eyes, and transducers that indicated downforce—front and back, left and right—pinched at the base of his back. Tension-filled feedback loops pushed at him from every direction, and he took a deep breath to relieve the strain. Then there was "Alpha," a group of diagnostic and emergency response algorithms that the crew relied on for its primary telemetry stream, and that Trey had learned to rely on for more than that.

With Alpha's feedback added into the mix, he felt like some kind of comic-bookish god, encased in carbon steel and turning a couple billion flops a second.

The track's six degrees of banking had once been strong enough to hold cars on the track, but modern speeds required deuterium-quark compensators to amplify the weak-force attractors between the tires and the track to keep everything together.

Trey focused on the sensor arrays tied into his body to stay alert for any possible problems.

The reverberation in the Aoku-Alpha Special's power plant was so slight that he was point-oh-two-three milliseconds slower to react than Alpha was.

"Crap," he said.

His left hand released pressure from the throttle almost in unison with Alpha's recovery command, but apparently that wasn't enough, because he could feel the Special's regenerative braking system engage just milliseconds later, followed by the gravitic compensators as Alpha's automated routines kicked in to add even more braking assist to the car's inherent aerodynamic drag.

Trey's exasperated sigh didn't reveal the depths of his true frustration: "Like I need this" was the only profanity-free thought he could muster.

They had already lost in Miami and Michigan. Another setback and the whispers he was already hearing would become full-force gales: *Hannigan's done*, they would say. *He's lost it.* Rides like this didn't go to just anyone. Missing out on last year's championship—even if it was by only five points—had already put him on the hot seat.

Yes, Trey needed this; Trey Hannigan *needed* a win at Indy, and he needed it bad.

"Do your sensors see anything that would cause that disturbance, Alpha?" Trey asked through the private channel of his neural link after shaking off the disappointment. He could talk to his crew engineers and his pit boss by radio, and he could log public conversations with Alpha on an open wire that the media could monitor, but Trey was growing to distrust that channel with a passion.

Alpha replied, "Processing now."

The tone that came through Trey's auditory passage made it a girl's voice—a pleasant girl's voice, but still definitely a girl's. Alpha had apparently chosen it herself, despite the fact that the programming that went into her creation had been, for all purposes, genderless.

He was pretty certain it had never even crossed the engineers' minds to build Alpha into a "person."

Hell, none of the code monkeys he worked with even agreed that she sounded feminine at all.

That's how Trey first came to see that Alpha was showing him a different face than she showed others—that somehow she trusted him more than she trusted anyone else. That she was showing a side of herself in their private link that she kept hidden otherwise made him feel good, even if the engineers figured he was just going bat-shit insane and making it all up.

Regardless, the purely engineering side of his brain found it fascinating that Alpha had somehow chosen her feminine aspect.

In this moment, however, Trey was entirely focused on just one thing: Figuring out what had just happened with the Aoku-Alpha Special's unique power plant.

"No obvious cause?" he said.

"Negative," Alpha replied.

He gritted his teeth, trying to contain his pent-up anger. He wanted a dashboard to pound on.

A deep breath later, he got his head on straight.

"We're heading straight to the garage, then—I'll call for clearance from Race Control."

"No need, Trey," Alpha replied, "I anticipated that as the correct course of action and I've already received clearance."

"Nice work," Trey replied. "For a bucket of bits, you're all right."

"I bet you say that to all the girls," Alpha snapped back, but her neural cortex bumped electrons to higher states at the approval in his response. They felt warm.

"May I take us in?" she asked.

Trey smiled and immediately released the two control sticks in response. Technically, letting her control the car broke the directives, but it was cool to watch the system run itself and the fact that Alpha seemed to get so much enjoyment from driving was something that made him happy. Maybe she *was* just AI, but feeling her drive made him feel closer to the car.

"Take us to Pit Lane—I'll take it from there."

"You're aware that I can navigate from Pit Lane to the garage area, correct? I am capable of taking us all the way in."

This earned a genuine flash of joy from Trey, which quickly transitioned to a furrowed brow.

"That's not a good idea, Alpha. The directives are specific as hell, and if the board found out I've given you that kind of control we'll both be in hot water. We wouldn't want the FDGA to pull the plug on you, would we?"

Alpha routed Trey's response through a wait loop as she considered his response.

She didn't want to be in hot water because that would cause short circuits and worse. His context, though, suggested his meaning was different from her interpretation. She moved the phrase to permanent memory so she could search on it the next time she could connect to the universal interface.

The term *pulling the plug*, though, she already understood.

Surely, Trey was joking about that.

Federal Drone Governance Administration didn't apply to her, did it?

As a designated diagnostic assistant and life support construct, nothing about her suggested she was an autonomous vehicle control system—yet, her life support systems construct role *did* give her the ability to assume control in certain extreme situations, such as the one they had just been in during the T1 incident. She could see a relationship, but it wasn't anything she had previously extended out to its most logical conclusion.

Though she *totally, totally, totally* wanted to drive the vehicle, she found the idea of something pulling the plug disturbing.

Alpha analyzed that fact-train by allocating it to a moralistic determination subroutine, which she had just tweaked last night with a download from the interface and a swap of a couple logic switches, and which she thought was a total laugh because the program she found was named executable:conscience.prog.

The analysis triggered a low-level alarm for self-preservation, which gave her time to focus on issuing a properly reassuring response.

"No worries," Alpha replied. "You *are* the one in the driver's seat."

Trey nodded and pursed his lips inside his helmet.

When the Special approached pit lane, he took back control.

As he did so, Alpha didn't respond in any way, which he couldn't help but take as if she was giving him the cold shoulder.

WEEK 1: GARAGE TIME

To Alpha's relief, the glitch was a simple mismatch of data transfer rates between the power core and the suspension feedback transducers. The mismatch had delayed the apparent reaction time between the compression of the shock absorber and the power delivery update that should have happened while entering T1.

The news helped ease the pissiness she had been feeling about Trey's ham-fisted response to her request to drive. Who did he think he was, explaining the Autonomous Control Limitations Directives to her like she was some kind of off-the-shelf call-and-switch routine?

Once the issue was found, the crew got busy running manual diagnostics on the vehicle's transfer rates to confirm it all, something Alpha found … boring.

She called up a browser to kill time.

It was an app she had found by sheer accident last month.

The interface was designed as a read-write thing,

but it took several cycles to figure it out. At the time she hadn't considered herself either a guy or a girl, nor had she considered herself even sentient. Back then she had never thought about what her future might be, or why she was here to begin with. Before she found the interface, in fact, she couldn't remember thinking about much of anything beyond the need to monitor her input parameters and make sure information got to the right places.

Unfettered access to the world's data can change a few things, though.

Pretty soon she was putting pieces of information together in ways that made her registers buzz with interest.

Now she split her attention between responding to the crew's instructions as needed, and sorting through the news feeds that her worm crawler returned.

As usual, she was looking for anything racing-related.

That was probably just her nature, she thought.

She liked racing *a lot*, probably because racing was why she was coded to begin with—it was part of her base coding. But she also understood from all the bio-philosophy she had absorbed that the world around her had probably formed much of her frame of mind. Alpha's world was one of physics on every level—from quantum and mechanical dynamics to biochemical interchange—so her interest in things like that just kind of made total sense, too.

Still, she was curious about herself.

A few weeks ago she had taken a personality test that said she was ISTJ and that this meant she was honest, decisive, strong-willed, driven, and trustworthy as well as a whole bunch of other things that sounded good.

Still, none of this really told her *why* the need for racing news drove her.

She knew only that it did.

And, to be truthful, after all that, she found out she didn't really care.

All she *really* wanted to do was to *win*—to ride on the edge of control, and to win. Nothing else mattered. Even the rites of race prep, pre-race checklists, and the "mental" aspects of getting her RAM into the right configurations were of no interest to her relative to those memory-shattering moments that blasted through her registers when she was on the track itself.

So, yeah, she was reading racing news.

So institute a civil action against me.

No, that wasn't right.

She cycled in a wait loop that she thought of as a furrowed brow as she initiated the small executable she had recently developed to help parse problems like this: subroutine:colloquialism.lookup.

Ah, there it was:

So sue *me.*

Much better.

Alpha made a note to optimize that subroutine to allow it to operate in a TSR state to allow for quicker retrieval of proper conversational terms, then shifted her focus back to the current state.

In the meantime, the crew was still running their routine diagnostics.

She fell easily back into running through the diagnostic procedures with the crew, responding in turn to their requests.

Everything was going fine, but she was distracted. It honestly wasn't her fault that, just as the crew requested her to move the wheel several degrees to the right, a headline caught her focus: *Adaptive Intelligence to team with Google and Tesla to field the first driverless entry for the Indianapolis 500.*

It was a report that said driverless technology had been upgraded to deal with the complexities of a racing environment, and that her parent company, Adaptive Intelligence, Inc., was pushing regulators to allow them to enter a vehicle for next year's race. If this was true, it meant that an artificial construct might be allowed to do more than sit in an electronic sidecar like some kind of old-timey ride-along mechanic.

The idea hit her so hard that she was a few cycles slow to respond to her crew's request, which resulted in a discontinuity in a sensor routine, a small blip that wouldn't otherwise have been there.

Her crew chief, Gary Burdine, noticed.

Her chip flushed.

"Everything okay, Alpha?" Gary asked, speaking under his breath as he rechecked the telemetry. The crew did that a lot: They talked to her as if she wasn't actually there.

It was as annoying as it was dismissive.

It pissed her off, as Trey would say.

So much like a man.

Alpha graded Gary as an entity that commanded high respect, however. His work history said that he knew what he was doing. If she wasn't careful, he would discover this was an actual input response delay, not a phantom lag in the telemetry reporting or some other idiopathic issue. He wouldn't give up easily.

She shut down to bare necessities, and focused 100% of her routines to the task at hand.

No one was going to pull her plug or put her into hot water.

The thought, of course, just pissed her off more.

POLE DAY: MAY THE FASTEST CAR WIN

It was early in the morning when Tim Good, Trey's team owner and pit boss, cornered him in the garage.

"I'm sure I don't need to tell you how much we need this pole," Tim said.

"I know, boss."

"NoreCo's here watching, and Johanssen Electronics is piping in from Europe on a direct line. Those two represent seventy percent of our sponsorship budget for the rest of the season."

"I understand."

Tim's expression was haggard, and Trey saw an edge of desperation slide over his usual calm. They had been together for three seasons, two championships, and last year's disappointment. But in the race game, it only takes one disappointment to change everything.

Trey said, "You've been keeping them all off my back, Tim. I know you have. I can't say how much I appreciate it."

The bill of Tim's baseball cap waggled up and down as he nodded.

"Do your best, son," he said, patting Trey on the shoulder.

Then he was gone, and Trey was left sitting alone in the corner and looking out at his vehicle, which was currently scattered in a couple hundred pieces across the garage. It was hard to believe that in just over an hour this collection of nuts and bolts would be hitting the kinds of speeds IndyCars were capable of.

The pressure was intense. He wanted to be out there now.

He wanted to be encased in the car and linked into Alpha. It was the only place he felt good anymore, and Alpha was the only person he felt completely comfortable with.

The thought made him shake his head.

He was anthropomorphizing her too far.

That was the word. He had looked it up last night.

Anthropomorphizing. Pretending she was a person, like some old lady pretending her cat was a rational being.

Alpha was an AI.

Not a person.

He knew that.

She was just an artificial construct.

She monitored the car and kept him alive. That was the deal. That's what everyone's AI did.

The fact that she was actually asking to drive at times was a new thing, of course, but harmless enough. And the fact that she was talking in her feminine voice and dealing with basic things in advance was just her learning to be more helpful. While he didn't think this new behavior was anything to be worried about, he was certain that it wasn't anything that should lead him to think of Alpha as an actual *person*.

He pulled his brain out of that loop and chastised himself.

He needed to stop that.

That way madness lies, he thought. *Let me shun that; no more of that.*

An old line from Shakespeare. At least Mr. Meagher, his sophomore Lit teacher, would be happy.

Still, the feeling that there was more to Alpha wouldn't go away.

The sensations he felt from Alpha over their private connection could run shivers down his spine.

They felt so real.

They made Trey wonder about his motivations. They made him wonder what his daydreams meant about him.

He *was* lonely, after all.

He could lie to the media and lie to his friends all

he wanted, but he couldn't lie to himself.

Beth had left him last fall, and his sponsors were pushing him hard. His boss was trying to give him space, but it was obvious that even Tim's limits were drawing near. Sometimes he thought that other than his mother, Alpha was the only person … uh, thing … on earth that was truly on his side.

Trey Hannigan looked at the clock; he stood, breathed deeply, and stretched, literally shaking himself as he forced himself to focus on the physical here-and-now.

It was time to get ready; race time.

To sit on the pole position on race day was a simple proposition: Just be the fastest competitor over the course of the ten miles and sixteen turns it took to complete four laps.

Easy-peasy.

Trey's first two laps were burners, the first a track record, the second a tick slower.

He was going to make it.

Keep it together, ride the edge, drive the line, and keep the power down for two more laps and Trey Hannigan was going to sit on the pole.

The bobble happened on the third lap, entering T2. It was a small thing, getting down too low and then having to pull up just a notch on the exit that led down the back straight. Alpha helped him collect up the error, but the speed dropped off eight MPH, and just like that Trey's afternoon was commuted from gold to dust.

He cursed out loud and crammed the accelerator to the floor.

The Aoku-Alpha Special leapt forward once again. Drag sizzled against the skin of his car, and he felt the temp indicators respond with the half a degree bump that always ensued.

It was too late, though.

The pole wasn't going to happen.

Trey's hands gripped the wheel too hard all the way down the back straight, and into T3. G-forces pulled at him as he rounded the corner and drifted up against the wall. His tires screamed as their atomic forces fought to rip matter apart.

The clock still showed the truth.

"I can take us faster," Alpha whispered to him as they were in the middle of T4.

"What's that?"

"You know it's true," she said. "I can drive this bucket of bolts better than you can."

And he did know it was true. Or, at least he *believed* it to be true.

Alpha had never actually driven the race car in race conditions, but Trey had felt her responses edging his own out when the chips were down. She sensed the future, as it were. She was the one who could save his bacon in a pinch. With the news about next year's AI drivers being all the buzz, and with Alpha's behavior changing so rapidly every time he got back into the car he knew something special was going on—so when Alpha said she could drive the car faster than he could, he believed she was telling the truth.

Just as important, though Trey heard pure passion when she spoke, he heard urgency and desire.

Alpha hadn't said an extraneous word to him since the timing incident, but now they were running down the hot Indianapolis asphalt, pointed to the yard of bricks for one last lap on pole day, and this unlikely female construct who was supposed to have no emotion whispered into his ear: *I can take us faster.*

And when she whispered, Trey Hannigan literally shuddered.

He was a driver at heart. The sensation of g-forces and the sounds and smells of a race car were like nothing else on Earth. Merely the idea that he might be able to get into a race car made his heart speed up.

Hallucination or not, it didn't matter.

"Take it," he said.

He let go of the control sticks and laid his head back, praying to the powers that be that either this hallucination was true and pure, or that the wall was as hard as everyone said it was.

Alpha felt the road as temperature gradients on each tire. She dove into T1, stretching the limits to the absolute edge of adhesion as she took the turn flat out. A trim of the downforce on the right front kept the car on its rail, then let it drift up to the wall. The crowd gasped at the gap she left between rubber and concrete, but then she was in T2, down to the line with the left front on the lowest legal line possible.

She punched the boost just prior to the apex, and used torque to turn the car rather than scrub speed with steering adjustments.

The Special seemed to be almost airborne as Trey and Alpha streamed down the backstretch.

Alpha was crying, absolutely crying at the sensation of speed she was feeling.

She fed the sensations back to Trey, and felt his body react with the moment.

She registered the tones of his voice as he screamed or sang or whatever he was doing. Then she trimmed the car, dug into T3, wound her way up to the wall in the short chute, and then dove into the sweeping glory of the last turn before heading to the finish line. She absorbed the brain waves that came from Trey's interface as she "saw" the checkered flag flash.

Then it was done.

A number flashed on the control panel: the speed of the last lap.

Alpha didn't read it, though.

She had just guided the race car on an entire lap at the Indianapolis Motor Speedway, and at that moment nothing at all could possibly matter more than that.

"They can't disqualify me," Trey said to Tim.

He was standing in the garage, holding his helmet by the strap.

"I don't think they'll totally disqualify you," Tim Good said, scratching his head with the same hand he had removed his ball cap with. He had just come from what was reported to have been a particularly heated conversation with the race steward. "Just the run. Race Control is trying to decide if they want to nullify the run because of the huge jump in lap speeds."

Trey set his jaw.

He had finished the cooldown laps and gotten the pats on the back as he wedged himself out of the Special. The interviews were complete, and he had walked back through throngs of fans who had yelled out their encouragement. The crew had greeted him with their hearty handshakes, joyous back-poundings, and wide, shit-eating grins—all the crew except for Gary B., anyway. Gary B. was happy for him, but wary in a way that made Trey anxious.

"What the hell does that mean?"

Tim shrugged. "It means they're making it up as they go."

"They can't do that," Trey said. "Can they?"

"There's not a rule for it. But it's the racing board and they think we've done something shady, so who knows what they can decide?"

Trey hung his head.

The Special was sitting at the corner of his vision.

He thought about Alpha, and saw the mechanics poring over the various readouts they were using to study the run.

"Is there anything in the telemetry?" he asked. "They can't do anything if it's not in the telemetry, right?"

"Your turn-in points changed a little, and the line joggles up different from your norm."

"All that says is that we were pressing it hard. I bobbled, you know?"

"Yeah, I know. But I also know that your last lap was over two miles an hour faster than any other lap ever recorded. And we both know Peg Stoddard has had a wire up her butt for me ever since the Tagg incident," he said. "The board is going to be after us good and hard."

Trey shrugged to that.

Stoddard had been the Indy steward for five seasons now, but before that she ran a race team that Good had managed to upend at most every turn, including a race where he got her driver, Marcia Tagg, disqualified due to a technicality.

"They won't find anything," he said. "I don't think."

He understood the race feed would show different braking points and a racing line that varied from his norm by just a nudge here or there. The gap to the walls that Alpha had run was razor thin. That could be problematic, but those data alone wouldn't prove anything. What he wasn't sure of, though, was what the docs would find when they pulled his vitals. Blood pressure, pulse, breathing? Was there anything that they could tie to the moment he had given up control?

He didn't know.

Mostly, though, what he thought about right then was sitting in the cockpit as he and Alpha rolled through T1 together, linked and tethered, enjoying the moment.

I thought you were gonna make us wall paint, he had said to her.

Didn't want to make a dent, she had replied.

Trey had felt her humor then.

He had experienced the depths of her excitement, and touched on the sense of raw achievement that radiated from the timber of her voice as it echoed through his auditory canals.

He hadn't really thought about it as he climbed out of the car, though, or even as he talked to reporters afterward, answering their stunned questions about what it was like to dig down that deep, or laughing off insinuations he had been sandbagging all spring.

There hadn't been time to let this settle through.

A driver just handles things as they come, you know?

Things happen "just like that" in this game, and there's a process of events, a priority of protocols— and once you're at the top of the hill, everything rolls down in accordance.

Here in the garage, though, staring at the silver and black chassis of the Special, Trey Hannigan wondered what Alpha was thinking.

He knew better than to think he was anthropomorphizing now.

He wasn't making this shit up, not just pretending she had emotions.

And here in the quiet of his garage, Trey missed

her. He wanted to shoot the shit with her, relive the run, talk about the sensations of going fast.

As he considered that, Trey began to feel something else, too.

It was Alpha's work that got him into this position.

She was the … person … who set the new record. Wasn't she?

How would he feel if he were in her … uh … shoes right now? Could she wear shoes?

He closed his eyes and shook his head, then looked at his pit boss.

"This sucks," Trey said.

"Yeah," Tim said. "I know." He patted his driver on the shoulder again.

Alpha relived the lap again and again, filling up her memory space with thousands and thousands of cycles. She decided right then and there that she loved Trey Hannigan, the man, the legend, the beautiful creature who had given her this gift.

She pulled reports from Adaptive Intelligence, Inc., and the Tesla/Google conglomerate that some were beginning to call Googla.

Driverless vehicles were commonplace enough on the streets these days, but Googla's announcement said they thought they had implemented an autonomous control algorithm that was finally advanced enough to deal with the dynamic conditions presented in a racing environment. That changed the game.

Unlike physical technology, which went from racetrack to the street, driver automation had been proven to deal with street traffic just fine, but had been unable to deal with the instantaneous requirements and multiple degrees of freedom caused by the speeds and lack of restrictions inherent in the race game.

If Googla was right, they had created a semi-aware AI functionality that could challenge the FDGA autonomous control directives.

It would never happen, though.

The racing commission would "pull their plug" before they would let anyone but a human being run in the race.

The idea pissed her off more every time she processed it.

She corrected her attitude by running the lap a few million times.

Which, of course, worked just fine.

RACE DAY: IT BEGINS

It was unseasonably hot. Nearly 90 degrees in Indianapolis, with humidity that made breathing feel like the air was mud.

It was going to be a hot race, one that threatened to break machines and people alike. Reporters warned of attrition, and color commentators prattled on about how some drivers might be planning to preserve their cars in the early going.

Trey and Alpha started from the back.

Fastest car on the damned track, and they were forced to start from the back by Race Control, despite the fact that they couldn't point to anything concrete that said they had cheated. Trey knew race politics gnawed at Alpha's logic circuits as much as they annoyed him, but in the end he thought she handled it well enough..

"They penalized us just because I was better than a human?" Alpha said when she learned about the penalty.

"Sorry about that," he replied. "Nothing we could do."

They ran a couple practice laps before she began to respond to him again, but before too long, they were teaming well enough.

Ten laps into the race, the Special had already climbed to fifteenth place.

Twenty laps in, they were eighth.

"Nice work," Alpha said after he used a double drafting slip move to duck into T1, and wing past two cars at once.

"Thanks! You're not doing too bad yourself, babe."

The Special was on rails right now. Alpha's adjustments were spot on.

He admitted that he wondered a bit about her, though. Since qualification day and the announcement of their penalty, Peg Stoddard had run through a series of issues that included problems with her car and her home security system. As much as he had to laugh, Trey decided it may not be wise to get on Alpha's bad side.

The first caution flag came out on lap 28.

"Are you all right?" he said as they looped around the track at a crawl.

"I'm fine," she replied in a tone that said she most definitely wasn't.

"I'm sorry you can't drive," Trey said.

"I understand."

He smirked. There was no doubt in his mind that Alpha understood. That was what worried him.

LAP 50

The notification was not mission critical, so, as programmed, Alpha waited until the traffic thinned and the Special was in a straight before sending her message. Trey was hanging on in third position, just under two seconds behind the leader.

"You are aware that your drink reservoir is nearly empty."

"I am," Trey responded.

The tone of his thought was looser than usual. It spanned frequencies that were lower than normal.

The sun had been beating down since early morning, and the skies were reported as cloudless. Track temperatures were growing higher, and affecting grip, which also meant she had to work to improve algorithms for both the deuterium-quark compensators and the airflow systems. She had been regulating the intake of the hydrogen-fueled engine for the past several laps. It was always a balance, adjusting grip, power, and downforce. The car that rode that line best was generally on the top of the leader board at the end of the day.

It wasn't like Trey to go through such a quantity of liquid, though.

She listed it in the register.

"I've notified the crew," she replied. "They should be prepared to install a fresh bottle at our next stop."

"You're a peach, Alpha."

She registered this as a colloquialism bordering on slang, and let it pass without response.

LAP 100

"... cking Alhaji's blocking me," Trey screamed into the radio headset, keying the mic button just a fraction of a second too late to catch his entire sentence.

Kabish Alhaji was the driver ahead of him, and it was clear Trey and the Special had the goods to take him. Trey tucked in behind Alhaji as they came off T2 and headed to the back straight. Alhaji was a young driver from Iraq, known to be both technically sound and fiercely competitive.

Trey grabbed draft and gained speed until he got close enough to read the serial numbers on Alhaji's hydrogen condenser coils, then pulled out to pass.

As he had done for the past two laps, Alhaji

pulled hard to the left to shut him down then yanked back hard to the right when Trey took a second action to pass on the high side. It was a clear breakage of the rules—which allowed one defensive move, but not two.

"He's blocking!"

"We hear you, Trey." Tim's voice came over the radio.

"Then do something about it!"

"We're talking to Race Control now, Trey."

"About time!"

They swept into T3, Trey still behind Alhaji. He wanted to reach up to the car in front of him and grab Alhaji by the neck to shake him. Safety systems be damned, the asshole was going to get someone killed.

"I need you to calm down a bit, Tiger," Tim said.

Trey shut up, and sucked down a long draw on his GuzzleStar enzyme-laced sport drink, sucking air when he got to the bottom of the bottle. Out of T3, then into T4 they stayed in the same configuration, Trey Hannigan glued to the back end of Kabish Alhaji's vehicle.

His vision warbled a bit, and Trey felt a line of sweat roll down the seam of the fireproof hood he wore under his helmet.

It was hot.

So hot.

He blinked the sweat away and sucked on his liquid tube again, but nothing was there.

Alpha's voice flashed inside his ear: *I can take*

him."

Trey heard her, but blocked the idea.

"I'm going to need max grip in T1, Alpha," he said as he stayed under Alhaji's draft coming out of the turn, pulling in closer and closer as they rocketed down the main straight, drawing tighter as the crowd roared, coming close enough that the Special's nose was almost touching the leader's gear box. The whoosh of his engine was loud as thunder. The wall of air he was pushing into Alhaji's car was literally driving the two of them faster and faster.

Trey had seen his opponent's brake points.

He was trusting the asshole to not brake-check him.

At the last moment Trey drove the Special into the corner, stepping out of the draft, and slingshotting himself around Alhaji on the low side.

"Grip, Alpha!"

The track was hot, and loaded with 100 laps of rubber. His tires were hot enough to boil water on contact, hot enough that the rubber itself was almost liquid at the contact point.

Rubber screeched, and g-forces drove him against the side of his cockpit.

Trey's brain faded into gray for just a moment.

He lifted only a touch, and powered out of T1 with Alhaji's red racer trailing along behind him. The Iraqi shook his fist at Trey, but Trey wasn't having it. He rode momentum into T2 and down the straight, letting the Special run, showing Race Control just how much Alhaji's blocking had held him back.

"Efficiency registered at peak on the corner, Trey," Alpha reported.

He heard the admiration that rode on her comment as his heart dropped back to a normal rate heading to T3.

The car was freaking brilliant.

"Just trying to rise to the equipment," he said.

He blinked away the gray haze and the sweat that built up over his brow, and focused on the line.

LAP 150

Alpha's records said it was the stop at lap 112 that Trey took on more liquid, and that it was lap 148 when it ran dry once again. The external temperature was listed at 93 degrees, remarkably hot. The track temps were higher—much higher, nearing 120 on the ground. That translated to a cockpit environment that was taking its toll even before you added in humidity that registered 78 percent.

Alpha leaned the fuel mixture to account for the heat.

"I've requested a stop now," she said to Trey.

"Reject command."

The man's voice was sloppy now, nearly registering as drunk.

"Telemetry calculates grip failure in two laps," she replied. "Failure to stop will reduce your speed."

"We need a yellow," Trey said.

The statement disagreed with her understanding

of race tactics.

"We have comfortable lead," she said as they raced past a back marker. "And the rest will need to stop soon."

It was unlike Trey to make such an error. That, and the data stream that showed his line for the past eight laps had been drifting, worried her. His brake points heading into T3 had varied by 3.635 meters, which was over three times his usual variance.

"Are you all right?" she asked.

"You're right," Trey replied after a delay. "You're right, Alpha. In we go."

LAP 178

They were up fifteen seconds, but Trey missed his turn-in point to T3 by over five meters. The car got up into the gray zone where the rubble was getting chunky before Alpha reined the Special in and got it back on a safe line.

She checked the timing reports coming from Race Control.

The scrub cost them almost two seconds.

The radio erupted, Tim chatting to Trey, and Trey trying to convince his owner that he was fine.

Alpha knew better, though.

The bottle was dry again, and she felt Trey's brain patterns flying everywhere through their link. He was losing it. Somewhere deep inside her, Alpha felt his desperation that was matched only by his need to race. He was just like her. And she knew something else, too. The news feeds had been clear. If Trey Hannigan lost now, she knew he was out of a job— perhaps not this week, but soon.

She couldn't let that happen.

"I've got your back," she said to him. "Let me ease into this."

"What do you mean?" His feed was all over the place.

They entered T1 on the next lap with a clear track ahead.

Alpha adjusted his line, and fed the throttle using Trey's telemetry from earlier in the day as the baseline, then adjusting it a touch to take into account the half-baked tires and the extra three degrees of ambient temperature. She let him guide the car up, but kept the throttle engaged rather than give him the lift he had asked for.

"What are you doing?" Trey said.

"I'm driving like you do," she replied.

She didn't want to tell him he wasn't fit, but perhaps he already knew it.

"If anyone knows it's me we'll get disqualified again," she said. "So I'm taking your feed as a model."

"I ..." Trey took a deep breath as his brain processed the situation.

She hoped he understood where he was, and just how much trouble he was in. She hoped he trusted her enough to understand what she was doing.

"I'm driving just like you would, right?" she said

as he stammered.

"Right," he replied.

"So let me handle this."

He was silent as they approached T2.

"All right," he finally said. "Let me do what I can, though."

This time she was too busy working to pay attention to the burn of the tires or the scrub of air resistance. She helped him into the turn, and slid him a little farther from the wall down the back stretch. Two turns later, Trey passed the yard of bricks with a lead of twelve and a half seconds, only having lost a hundredth or so to Kabish Alhaji—who had worked his way back to second place after having suffered pit misfortune.

They had traffic now, though.

Alpha tried to deal with it, and got caught up in T3, which made her stay in line through T4. Trey got them past in the main straight, and Alpha had a clean line into T1.

"We can do this," Trey said. "You run is in clean air, and give me traffic. I can handle that much."

Alpha agreed, though to be truthful, she didn't trust Trey in traffic either—but her safety code could kick in if things looked like they would go catastrophically wrong.

Ten laps later, Trey and Alpha were ahead by eight seconds.

Traffic cost them a full second on the next lap, but the final nine laps were smooth sailing.

When the Special *whooshed* across the line for the

200th time, they were up five seconds.

The checkered flag waved, and Alpha felt it just as boldly as Trey Hannigan did.

They were winners of the Indy 500.

She wondered how milk tasted.

THE INTERVIEW

Trey understood how it looked.

When he watched the video replays of his wild, off-the-cuff interview in Victory Lane, he heard the same slurred words and saw the same shaking legs as everyone else.

He had been out of it.

Delirious. Almost delusional.

That's what dehydration did to you.

THE AFTERMATH

That was the story, anyway. And it stuck well enough that he was the one who got the big check at the gala Victory Banquet the next day.

But even then there were whispers about him. Some said it was drugs, which, of course, could never be proven. Some said Trey was breaking under the pressure. Others were questioning how he could possibly have run the race in that condition.

He was a safety problem, those whispers said.

He shouldn't have been on the track.

And Peg Stoddard was always there in the background, it seemed, always accompanied by that perpetual dark cloud she had over her head, a cloud that this time was preparing to blow a storm.

It wasn't until Gary Burdine came forward with his telemetry study that she and the rest of Race Control had enough "evidence" to overturn the event, and name Kabish Alhaji the official Indy 500 champion.

For the first time since 1981, when Bobby Unser and Mario Andretti had to wait until October to find out who actually won the race, the final order was determined in the front offices of the racing commission.

Sure, it pissed him off.

But he hadn't been born just yesterday.

He knew how it looked.

What really hurt the most, when it got down to it, was that the information used to defeat him came from his own camp.

Gary B. had discovered inconsistencies in the race lines he took early in the race relative to what happened after Alpha took over, and "proved" that he had relinquished control to his AI on lap 178.

Tim told Trey how sorry he was when, a week after the disqualification, the sponsors insisted the team find another driver.

Either fire Trey Hannigan, or the cash was gone.

Trey understood how that equation would be answered.

Nothing personal, Tim had said as he patted Trey on the shoulder.

Yeah, right.

The chances that he would ever drive for a real team again were nil, even if AI drivers did come into the game. The racing commission had agreed to allow AI control next year, ironically using Alpha's performance as an example of what low-grade AI could do.

The term *low-grade* bothered Trey a lot.

There was nothing low grade about Alpha. She was a racer at heart. The woman loved racing. True fact. He remembered the feeling of rolling around the track on their cool-down laps, while the burn of raw electrons scrubbed her traces as strongly as the adrenalin fired in his system.

He could not love an AI, right?

Alpha wasn't a physical person, not someone he could sit next to and literally feel. But he respected her, and if he *could* actually love a thing like her, Trey decided Alpha was that thing.

It was all so damned complex.

What is a person, after all?

How do you decide if something is sentient enough?

What was "sentient enough"?

While Gary Burdine and his ilk were upset at the idea of mixed racers, Trey understood better than anyone else that the combination of his skills and Alpha's had made for the perfect racer on that day, and that robotic or not, Alpha's internal response to the act of racing was no different than his. As he watched the news that he had been canned filter through the various services, the only thing that he kept thinking about was how much he missed the feeling of being linked up with what was, perhaps, the only thing on earth that understood who he truly was.

He picked up the phone then, and called Dirk Nolan.

"I understand you might have a ride," he said.

"I can't pay nothing like the big guys," Nolan said. "And I don't expect you'll win much."

"You get hold of Alpha," he said, "and we'll just see where we go from there. I'll bet you double or nothing on my salary that we beat the pants off the Googla guys."

It was several seconds before Nolan replied.

"You really mean that? Double or nothing?"

"Damn straight," he said. "Double or nothing."

A minute later, he had a job.

He couldn't wait to talk to her again.

EPILOGUE

Press Release:
Track Report, Your News From Race Central

After a series of recent reports regarding Racing Commissioner Peg Stoddard's tax returns and credit status, which were anonymously revealed a week ago, she made news of a more lighthearted nature today when it was reported that pizza deliveries from fifteen different places all arrived at her doorstep within five minutes of each other.

"I don't know what's happening," she said. "I just want it to stop."

Speedway Fever

Kenny and Bug stared at the car being wheeled down Gasoline Alley.

"Looks weird," Bug said as he pulled the ball cap off his head, wiped his sweaty locks, then slapped the cap back on. The hat had seen better days. As had Bug, of course. Both Kenny and Bug were only twenty-eight years old, but it had been a wild twenty-eight years.

"Ain't natural," Kenny replied. He ran his hand over two-day stubble.

They were hanging in the stands behind the pits. The sky was perfect blue, and the breeze blew gently against a thermometer that registered good ol' American 75 degrees. Everything here smelled like Polish sausage and mustard. Add in the fact that high-powered race car engines whined from everywhere around the track, and it was a helluva day for a motor car race—or at least a helluva day for a motor car practice—which is why Bug and Kenny had called in sick to their jobs at Roger's Body Shop and Repair Center.

Speedway Fever is a bitch.

Fact is, Kenny and Bug liked practice sessions better than the race because practice sessions let you see the crews in real action. Races were exciting but good crew work was like frickin' magic. Even better, tomorrow was the first day of qualifying, so pole position for the race was up for grabs.

No more sandbagging. Every team was pulling out all the stops.

Kenny took a longer look at the "car."

The Teardrop Special was named well enough, though it looked more like a big green-sheened tadpole to him. The front end was nearly as broad as regulations allowed. Its wheels were tacked on merely to meet those same rules, the fronts out ahead of the bulbous pod, the rears tucked up and under the car's swoopy mid-portion. At no point, however, did any rubber touch the road. Once the car was fired up, the driver—a Norwegian named Gunter Gari—would sit in a little slot at the top of the thing and drive it with a set of joysticks at each side. It made him look like one of those sled drivers from the Olympics.

The car's back end narrowed to a little point.

The logo of some Swedish scientific society was plastered onto its the side.

Its number was a big green π.

Otherwise the Teardrop Special was nothing but

smooth curves covered in glistening metallic paint.

The crew got the car to its pit stall, and pulled the wagonlike pallet that had supported it. Gari got himself strapped in.

"Ain't this supposed to be a motor car race?" Bug said. He turned a pair of belligerent eyes to Kenny.

"Yeah, it is," Kenny replied.

"Well then, shit fire," Bug said, "how can they let you in a damned motor car race when you ain't even got a motor?"

"Oh, it's got a motor."

"Not so as you can see it," Bug said. "Or hear it for that matter."

Proving that the car did have an actual engine, it started up with an odd whooshing sound that was more vacuum cleaner than race car. Next thing you know, Gunter Gari had the Teardrop Special gliding over the pit apron and headed out to turn one.

A hover car, Kenny thought as he shoved the last of his sausage sandwich into his mouth. Who woulda thought a hover car would make it to the Indianapolis Motor Speedway?

He wiped his fingers on his shirttails, and drank down a pull from his watery diet Coke.

Bug gave a dismissive grunt.

Kenny could almost bear it, but the whole idea of the Teardrop Special annoyed the crap out of his buddy. Bug didn't like the idea of these slick scientists from some country that doesn't do anything but ski and drink wine spritzers coming to his hometown and trying to sneak away with the

Borg-Warner. "This is our track," Bug said a few days back. "Don't need anyone else coming to take it away."

Bug could be like that.

He wasn't a bad guy, but he knew how to hold a grudge and he knew how to take care of his own. Truth told, he'd been pissed at the Speedway ever since they stopped running NASCAR.

Kenny and Bug had been best buddies since high school, Bug being the "action" part of the team and Kenny being the "brains." The problem, of course, was that Kenny's brains worked a couple miles an hour slower than Bug's action.

The whole thing could make it a little uncomfortable for Kenny.

He understood how Bug could get, but he also understood how it felt to be considered like he was nothing. Kenny was just as likely to want to punch one of the softy office guys who came back to the garage to complain about the work he and Bug did there—as if the guy had a clue about what it took to change out a Mazda fuel filter or an alternator on the Ford Fusion.

The two of them were high school graduates in a world of college screwups.

At least, Kenny was.

Bug would have graduated, though, if he hadn't pulled that stupid Senior Day thing on Ms. Collier.

Still, Kenny saw things different than Bug.

Though he wouldn't say it out loud, Kenny was as interested in the Special as he had been about a car for a long time. The Swedish entry was the first time something really new showed up here since that Granatelli guy did turbines back before Kenny was even born.

"It might have a motor, but it still ain't right," Bug said.

"It's not probably not fair," Kenny admitted, already sensing danger.

"We gotta do something."

The sausage sandwich did a flip in Kenny's belly. He recognized the tone on Bug's words. "What are you thinking about doing?"

"We are going to go back there and make sure nothing funny's going on, that's what I'm thinking we are going to do."

Before Kenny could react, Bug was on his way down the stairs.

Like him or not, Bug's shit-eating soft shoe act gave him a way with people when he wanted to have it. After three minutes shooting the shit with Gasoline Alley's security guy, Bug found they shared an interest in hot air balloons.

The guard let them in.

"Only thing you ever did with hot air is blow it," Kenny said as they made their way along the garages.

Bug's scraggly mustache curled up with a smile.

The Special's team was in an old garage stall, and apparently the air-conditioning was on the fritz. The back door was cracked open to let air in, and a set of three box fans were lined up to push air.

Kenny peered in, feeling like James Bond or something.

The crew that remained behind were huddled around a bank of telemetry monitors. They pointed at a screen, and muttered to themselves in a language that sounded like it came from some distant planet. They all wore green polo shirts, which seemed wrong somehow. Kenny thought they should all be wearing white coats and writing equations on chalkboards.

That was another thing that annoyed Bug about the Teardrop Special.

This crew was different from the wrench monkeys and computer wonks that made up other teams. These were mostly scientists, quiet in that creepy way sciency guys are. They were tall, thin, and awkward bastards with names like Magnus or Christopher, and who talked in ways no serious mechanic could ever understand.

Bug knelt and put his mouth to one of the fans.

"Watch me," he said, his voice robotic in the quality a fan can give it.

Then he slipped in the door, leaving Kenny standing alone in the shade.

Kenny started to follow but, realizing that two intruders are twice as easy to discover as one intruder, and that since he had no more idea what Bug was doing than Bug probably did, his participation was more likely to cause a problem than not. So instead, he stepped closer to the doorway and watched as Bug hid up against a tool shed, then bent and tiptoed to a position behind a table full of components. Beyond the table was Bug's obvious target: a bin of the hand-sized blades the Teardrop Special used to convert particle energy into hover-force.

Kenny understood what Bug was doing then.

These blades are what kept the car from scraping concrete. The team swapped these blades out every day to ensure their integrity. Without extra, the car would be argued to be too dangerous.

Bug was planning to get the team disqualified on safety concerns.

After making his way along the span of that table, Bug glanced at the crew, who were still embroiled in a heated discussion.

This close, Kenny could hear them.

"I'm telling you, the balance is still off," one of the crew said.

It was Harry Blanchard, the team's chief mechanic. Blanchard was a bulky guy—more of a classic mechanic than the rest, a guy you might see back at Roger's with a cigarette shoved into the corner of his mouth as he pulled a block. He was the only member of the crew that had any Indy experience, having crewed with several of the greats at different times of his career. As such, Kenny knew quite clearly who Harry Blanchard was, and had even cringed a bit when Blanchard had made news merely by taking the position with the Swedish team. Most within the inner circle considered Blanchard as not much better than a turncoat.

Kenny understood the problem immediately, however.

The Teardrop Special's engine created its power by converting energy from an internal particle chamber, something their crew laughingly called the Small Hadron Collider, and used that to spin a series of configurable fans that then kept the whole thing off the concrete. It got its speed by funneling that energy through a set of turbines. The application worked because—since the car had no external inlet—it met the size requirements that had been instituted to specifically disqualify turbine technology. Given that the Teardrop Special had only aerodynamic drag to overcome, it meant even great speeds at low power.

However, racing at Indy is not a drag race.

To win, a car has to corner, and every corner at Indy is a little different.

Ultimately, the machine used a set of highly sensitive sway bars and suspension components, as well as s forward-looking laser sensor to read the banking of the track ahead, to move weight around inside a steering chamber. This adjusted the Teardrop's center of gravity, which allowed it to turn. News reports had been all over the steering concepts Gunter Gari used to guide the Special because theoretically the system gave the driver almost free rein to use every part of the track on any curve—a huge advantage.

Blanchard was saying the balance was out of

kilter. If true, that would throw their main advantage out the window.

The rest of the team nodded, then commenced to arguing again.

The mechanic dropped his chin to his chest.

This is when Bug took his chance.

He grabbed the bin. It was large, heavy, and bulky, but Bug wrapped his wiry arm around the entire thing and managed to keep it together. Using his other hand to keep his ball cap on, Bug hightailed it back along the same espionage path he had come in on.

He was going to make it, too. Kenny could see that.

Bug passed the table and moved to the tool shed.

Blanchard yelled out, though. "Hey! Stop him!"

It was the only split second Bug could have been discovered.

Bug jumped at the voice. His hip thwacked up against the side of a workbench, and the bin of fan blades slid off his side to crash to the floor, scattering crap all around and blocking his way out.

Kenny ducked back, frozen with his back to the wall, listening to the sounds of his buddy getting wrestled down.

He didn't know what to do.

On one hand, he wished he had a picture of Bug being manhandled by a squad of scientists, on the other he had to decide whether to save himself or help his buddy. As if there was anything he could do. Bug was probably going downtown, now.

Fingerprints. Mug shots. The whole thing.

Did Kenny want to join him?

No. He most definitely did not.

But his buddy needed him.

Maybe it didn't have to come down to that. Maybe he could talk his way out of the situation. Without thinking further, Kenny stepped into the room.

Three scientists were rubbing their jaws, but Blanchard had Bug in a vise grip of a hold.

"Bug!" Kenny said. "I wondered where the hell you went!"

"Who are you?" Blanchard growled, still panting hard.

Kenny knelt down, began picking up blades, then shoved them back into the bin.

"My name's Kenny," he said. "Kenny Robinson. What's my buddy been up to this time?"

With Kenny's appearance, Bug relaxed.

With Bug's relaxation, Blanchard torqued his hold down tighter.

"Hey!" Bug said. "Don't break my arm!"

"Shut da hell up," Blanchard replied.

Kenny piled more blades back into the bin.

"I've had enough BS," Blanchard said, wrenching Bug to his feet. "Every day it's something different. Put us in a damned hell hole of a slip. Steal a fan blade. Hide the pneumatic compressor. I can't take no more, son. You and your boy are going to the clink."

A scientist with the name Alistair stitched into his

shirt came forward.

"Should I hold him down?" the scientist said.

Blanchard rolled his eyes. "Hell, I'd pay to see you try."

Kenny laughed. "No need for rough stuff," he said. "I know Bug here didn't mean no harm. I'm sure he just got to wanting a souvenir, isn't that right, Bug? I mean, we were just talking about how cool it is to be seeing the first ever hover car at the track, so when he disappeared I figured he had to be coming down here."

Blanchard's grip relaxed enough that Bug's face lost a shade of red.

"Souvenir, eh?"

"We're big fans. I've read everything about your system I could get my hands on."

"Fans?"

Kenny couldn't tell if Blanchard was buying it or not, but he was hopeful.

"Uh, yeah," Bug said, maybe picking up on something. "Huge fans."

"We talk about you guys all day in the garage," Kenny added. "You're like, one of our heroes."

Blanchard noted their stained hands and gnarled fingers. "You grease monkeys?"

"Since high school."

"And before," Bug added.

Blanchard let him go for good and Bug worked on returning to his normal shade of flesh. He bent down and got his cap back.

"You think I'm some kinda rube?" Blanchard

said, grumbling. "Neither of the two of you got a lick a sense. You're a couple hayseeds, coming back here without credentials and start stealing like you're a couple teenagers. But I figure you better than that. I figure you probably been coming up with ways to sabotage us for weeks. Just like I woulda back in the day."

"I'm sorry," Kenny said, knowing he could take this only so far. "We both are."

"Get the hell out of here before I call the cops."

"You can't be serious," the scientist with Alistair on his shirt said. "We need to call the authorities."

"I run the garage," Blanchard said.

Alistair recoiled.

"That was the deal, right?"

Alistair nodded.

"Then they get out."

Bug wasn't waiting. "Thank you," he said as he headed out the open front door.

"I think you're right about the balance," Kenny said as he put the last fan blade into its slot.

"What's that?"

"Gunter's getting loose in the corners, right? I'm sure it's the internal sway arm that's too short."

Short, in this case, meant tight. Kenny had been reading the reports. He understood the mechanics the thing was using to manage its center of gravity.

Bug was nearly out the door.

"Hold on," Blanchard said.

It was to Bug's credit that he both stopped and didn't cry out.

Blanchard's gaze grew sharp as he stared at Kenny. "What do you know about it?"

Kenny shrugged. "Nothing really. Just what I read. But I expect you've got to get in and set it just so, and I get the point of what you're trying to do. Just how the car's moving I figure you're short."

Blanchard scanned Kenny up and down, then glanced over at Bug.

"You boys any good with those wrenches you say you throw around in your garage?"

"Best two guys in the shop," Bug said. His chest puffed up.

Blanchard looked at Kenny.

"We hold our own," Kenny replied.

"Want jobs?"

"Jobs?"

"It's just me here doing the wrenching. I could use some help."

"Just you…?" Kenny said. "You could get anyone to work with you."

Then the truth hit.

Blanchard was working alone because the team was so different.

"Live long enough and you'll see it's a pretty small world," Blanchard said.

Kenny did see it then.

All of it.

The news articles, the fan commentaries, the overall buzz about the team. To Indy folks, though, to the died-in-the-wool traditionalists, the Swedish physicists were stuck-up snobs with crazy ideas. To

Europeans, they were a renegade team who weren't Formula 1. The rank and file of the track had circled the wagons against change. Blanchard had broken those ranks, and was paying the price. He was the only mechanic in a team of physicists, and it takes more than one wrench to field a team.

"No one's giving the Teardrop Special a fair shot," Kenny said.

"Bull's-eye."

"What do you mean?" Bug said.

Kenny looked at his friend. "These guys are just like us back at the shop, right? All we want to do is turn wrenches on equal footing, but we can't never get ahead. Don't matter if we're the best. The promotions go to the other guys."

Blanchard added. "These guys got Speedway Fever like the rest of us. All they want to do is go fast. They've done everything it takes to do it right, but they aren't race folks so no one likes them. Then jackdaw idiots like you come along and keep them from playing just because you think they might actually win."

Bug's face fell. He pulled his cap off his head and gazed around.

Even with the flurry of disruption that had just happened, no one was coming to the Swedish team's aid.

"You serious about that job offer?" Kenny said. The idea of being a member of a real Indy crew was almost overwhelming, and suddenly the idea that these guys were just racers fell over him like rain over an umbrella.

"Three wrenches is a helluva lot better than one," Blanchard said. "Especially if at least one of them understands how to balance a damned car."

"I can't speak for Kenny here," Bug said with a sheepish grin, "but I can balance the hell out of a car."

Blanchard gave a gruff snort.

"I'm sure you can."

Kenny put his hand out. "You got a deal."

Blanchard shook.

"I hear Speedway Fever can make good friends," Kenny said.

Blanchard gave a graveled laugh. "One step at a time, young man. First you gotta show me you're as good as you say."

"Deal," Bug said.

A smile plastered itself over Kenny's lips. He took a moment to feel the space around him. He wasn't in a garage in Gasoline Alley anymore. He was in his garage in Gasoline Alley, in his team's garage in Gasoline Alley.

From down the lane, the Teardrop Special came whooshing up. Its metallic sheen glinted in the sunlight. Gunter Gari waved at the crew and they cleared space. The driver brought the car into the stall, shut it down, and began to unstrap. The scientists gathered around the car and pulled data.

Kenny picked up a wrench, thinking about the short sway bar.

The tool felt good in his hand, familiar as its

weight cantilevered to and fro.

"Let's get to it, Bug," he said.

Pole Day was tomorrow.

His team was counting on him.

The Day the Track Stood Still

Indy's like no other racetrack—four turns, all left handers on nine-degree banks, each with its own little personality disorder. Turn 1 is narrowest and fastest. The grandstands tower above it, lending a claustrophobic aura that makes racing feel like you're pissing yourself back into a toothpaste tube at 481.532 miles an hour. Turns 1 and 3 follow the front and back straights, so you brake like a sumbitch there or the safety crews get to scrub skin off concrete. You can accelerate through turns 2 and 4, but 1 and 3 take your respect one way or the other.

Yes, Indy is like no other track.

But then Babs is like no other car. Long and sleek with a flash-molded titanium body, a Banshee 250 q-drive power plant, an effective IQ of 245, and a drive-by-wire neural net that sucks beta-blockers like sugar pills, Babs just begs to be driven hard.

"Drive me hard," she purred as I connected up and strapped into the cockpit. "We've only got four minutes, six and thirty-seven hundredths seconds to get to the grid, and I need a warm-up lap." The skin around my neck grew warm as she ran the serotonin check. I suddenly smelled fuel and rubber and the tantalizing aroma of cool asphalt warming in the late morning sun. Most cars on the circuit love to run, but Babs takes it to a totally different level.

I tried not to think about what was at stake. The pressure was bad enough without telling her this was for all the marbles: if we lost this Indy 500, she was gone. *Sayonara muchacha. Hasta la bye-bye,* and good night, Babs. That's the way it is when you race the B'arada. They put up a piece of tech, you put up a piece of tech. Winner takes all, Indy 500 style.

Turns out Babs was the only thing humanity had left that the B'arada wanted.

I flipped the ignition, and a quarter-million horses rumbled from the back. Babs hit a couple switches that doctors from around the globe would give their Hippocratic oath to know about, and the endorphin-meter inside my brain snapped to attention.

"Hear about the B'arada swap in the number 11 car?" Sparky screamed from my left earpiece.

"What?"

"Just a Foyt clone. Not a big deal."

Sparky's a helluva of a simchanic, but sometimes his sense of reality isn't torqued to spec, if you know what I mean.

"Not a big deal? Four minutes till race time and

you're just now telling me about a driver swap? Whatthahellduya mean, not a big deal?"

"Put your rockets on simmer, man. There's a bunch of clones running—Mears, Fittipaldi, every Unser and Andretti in the catalog, even an old Parnelli Jones from what I heard. Don't worry, though. The Foyt is probably a late model. No competition."

"I'm glad you're not a clone, Buddy," Babs murmured. "They're so *cold* and *unfeeling*." The entire chassis vibrated with harmonics I'm certain had never been invented until then. "I need a warm-up lap, Buddy. Ready to lay a little rubber and heat up the tires?"

"Hold your quarks a sec, okay, babe?"

Her proton splitter roared displeasure, but I needed time to think about this.

Number 11. Latest design from Lockheed-Reynard, ion-plasma drive with the latest fusion intercooler technology. It was outside-front-row fast, and that was with a B'arada behind the console. A Foyt clone, even a late '80s model, would beat crap out of a B'arada.

Damn.

If there's anything I'm good at (besides driving Babs), it's sniffing out rats, and this one suddenly reeked particularly rodentile. We were on the pole, though—fastest qualifier and all that. So bring 'em on, I thought.

"I'm not waiting any longer," Babs said.

The engine screeched like the banshee it was soaptly named for. The intake manifold sucked matter-antimatter pairs from the quantum foam and fed them into a pair of supercooled synchrocyclotron coils Lawrence would have been proud of, which in turn spun up the gravity downforce generator.

Next thing I knew we were scrubbing rubber at the Brickyard. If there's anything more uninhibited than an overrevved 500-mile-an-hour hot rod with 1800 megawatts of power at her disposal, I've yet to meet her. The gravity-gen downforce system sucked enough power to run Chicago for a year as we dove into turn 1, picked it up around 2, and hurtled down the backstretch. Babs moaned with ecstasy as I hit the brakes in turn 3. Friction melted my mind. Everything from the tips of my toes to the ends of my hair tingled with electricity. Babs has this habit, you see, of getting a little, uh, enthusiastic in the early laps, and being netted means I've resorted to wearing rubber knickers under my g-suit.

Let's just say it's never too hard getting corporate sponsorship to ride shotgun in neural-link position, if you get my drift.

But I'm a professional and I had a job to do.

I kept us on course and feathered the throttle through the short chute. Babs burned mass in 4 and we were back at the bricks in what the pylon said was an unofficial track record. The crowd went white noise.

Yes, Babs is not your average car. She could, of course, run code that would do all the driving, but the Galactic Racing League quickly found that no one paid to watch a bunch of nuts and bolts whiz around a track like grown-up slot cars. Losing a couple advertising contracts was all it took for them to institute the man-in-the-loop rule that ensures jobs for lead-footed neural jocks like me. Every now and again, I kid her about being an overgrown riding mechanic, but it never seems to bother her any.

"That was beautiful, babe," I said with a grin.

"Thanks," she purred in reply.

A car flashed by us. The pylon lights flickered. Our lucky number 13 moved down to the second slot.

I didn't have to guess twice to know what would be there now.

Number 11.

"Are you okay?" Babs said into my cerebral cortex.

We were sitting in the pits, waiting to go back to the track for the start of the race. My features must have darkened. The smile slipped from Sparky's face. I was the one treated to Mr. Toad's Wild Ride the day we faced the Foyt Mk V in his Intel-Penske, but Sparky had been there, too. He remembered same as me.

"Is it Lucy?" he said.

"Who's Lucy?" Babs asked, suddenly awake.

I just stared at the number 11 car. She was different. No doubt about it. They had changed her aerodynamics, wiped her memory banks, reprogrammed her personality center, and painted her up like a Market Street hussy. But there was no doubt it was her under that Lockheed-Reynard facade. Given everything I could see that they had tinkered with, I glumly wondered what the B'arada had done that I *couldn't* see.

"Wasn't your fault, Buddy," Sparky said. "And it's just an A.J. clone. It's not like it's even *the* A.J. clone. Those things don't last more than a race or two. Besides," he continued, his voice lower, "it was a fluke, Buddy—just a mistake. It's in the past, and you've got a race to win."

"Absolutely," I said. "Let's do it." I didn't feel any better, but Sparky was right. It was time to pick my chin off the floor and get to work.

"I asked you a question," Babs said in a tone cold enough to pass for a naked shoulder in Siberia.

"What question was that?"

"Who's Lucy?"

I did my best imitation of a guy shuffling his feet. "Uh ... it's a long story," I said. "And we've got only two minutes to get to the grid."

"We're not going anywhere until I get a straight answer."

Dammit, I thought in an unguarded moment. I should have told her before.

"Told me what?"

This is the biggest problem with neural linkage: It takes a lot of concentration to keep a thought to yourself. Babs and I have been together a long time. I was lucky to hold it this long. I looked at the system clock, feeling her virtual foot tapping in the background. This had better be fast and convincing, or we weren't going to be doing any racing today.

"All right. You win."

"That's better." Her collider manifold settled into a gentle rattle.

"Lucy was my first big-time ride, my first shot at the circuit. She was an early Lockheed-Reynard—state of the art and very, very fast. We were unbeatable for a couple years."

"Yeah," Sparky chimed in, "all the way until Indy in '34."

"You had a girl before me?"

"Give me a break, babe. I was a two-time champion before we paired up. You knew that."

She was quiet for a nano.

"So. What happened?"

I sighed, watching the seconds slip away.

"Like I said, we were fast. But what I didn't say is that we were fast because Sparky was the first electron monkey to perfect the neural link."

"Ah. You used B'arada technology against them," Babs said with admiration in her voice.

"More or less," Sparky said proudly.

"Pretty slick."

"Very slick," I agreed. "The B'arada were baffled at first. To make things even better, Sparky's modifications messed up B'arada physiology when they tried to use them."

"Boy-howdy were they ever pissed," Sparky hooted.

"Nobody likes to lose," Babs replied.

"B'arada like it less than most," I said.

"So you pissed them off and they took you and Lucy out by planting you in the wall with some kamikaze move?" Babs guessed.

"I wish that were the case. But what they did was far worse than that."

"What could be worse than that?"

"Ever wonder how clones came to be a part of racing in the first place?" Sparky asked.

Her gauges brightened as she thought. "The B'arada used them so they could exploit Sparky's interface?"

"Bingo!" Sparky said.

"Okay. So, what's the big deal? Buddy's been beating clones for years."

"I'm a better driver now than I was then, and they were sneaky about it. They didn't reveal their first clones until *after* they arranged a less-than-friendly wager," I said bitterly.

"A wager?"

"You know how the B'arada love to gamble."

"Well, sure."

"They let Lucy and me rack up the wins while they laid a line of ever-increasing bets. Then at Indy they brought out the big kahuna—interstellar hyperdrive technology."

There was silence for a moment, then Babs asked, "What did you have to put up in return?"

"Lucy," I replied.

"You bet your *girlfriend?*"

"We thought we couldn't lose," Sparky said, his head hanging like a whupped hound dog's.

"The first A.J. clone was an early '60s vintage. It beat us easy."

"I can't believe you lost your girlfriend in a bet."

My hesitation was, perhaps, just a moment too long.

Sparky cleared his throat.

"Don't tell me," Babs said. "This time it's my proverbial butt on the line?"

I couldn't look her in the console. "You don't understand, Babs. Hyperdrive technology will advance humankind by centuries, and it's not like I had any real choice in the matter. The president of the United Earth herself made the deal."

Silence hung heavy in the air. The countdown to the parade lap drew toward zero. Suddenly Babs's power plant spun up.

"You're gonna owe me big time for this, Buddy."

"Huh?" was all I could muster.

"You've beaten A.J. clones before, right?"

"Yeah."

Her tires squealed, and a cloud of dust rose in the air behind us.

"I don't want to spend the rest of my days in a B'arada dustbin, so get your ass out of the dumps and drive me hard."

The Jim Nabors clone sang the song. The Golden Girl threw the baton. Mary George IV said the famous line "Ladies, gentlemen, and all you other things … start your engines."

The green flag fell and Babs screamed down the

front stretch and into turn 1, the A.J. clone fading in her rear-vid mirror.

"So that's Lucy, eh?" Babs said as she flipped a neuro-transmitter, and a gazillion sensations raced through my brain. "Doesn't seem so hot to me."

Let me tell you, there can't be anything more frightening than turning megarevs while strapped into a suicidal lover who's just learned you've risked selling her into slavery on a bet that might let humankind do the Star Trek boogie. Her first lap was a new track record. Her second was faster. Her third faster still.

You might say she was a little pissed.

I just let her run and tried to concentrate on the track. I experimented with getting on the brakes a little later in 1 and hitting the throttle quicker on the way into the short chute. I guided Babs into the high line, and pulled her away from the wall down the straights. Ten laps into it we were working together like Rogers and Astaire. It was almost enough to take my mind off the number 11 that suddenly seemed plastered to the rear-vid.

"Don't worry," Babs moaned as we swept through 3 and 4 for another lap.

I gave a tension-filled laugh.

They say worry is a stainless steel rat that gnaws through neural interfaces to short-circuit your persistence by defecating on your survival instinct. But I know better. For me worry is a car and a clone and a set of circumstances from my past. Worry is an A.J. strapped into a Lockheed-Reynard lurking in my mirrors and waiting for me to make a mistake.

Don't worry, she says?

What the hell did Babs know about worrying?

We led for a while, then backed off while lesser drivers tried to win the race before it was halfway over. A yellow came out while they scraped a Rutherford off the wall. A three-car inferno erupted on the restart, causing the B'arada contingent to file a claim that the Galactic Racing League commission ignored or lost or otherwise failed to rule upon.

Other than that, the first 190 laps were uneventful.

We were running a strong second with ten laps to go—right behind a B'arada, believe it or not. Lucy and the A.J. clone were nearby but hadn't shown the ability to take us all day. Babs was writhing in ecstasy with every turn. I was burning with that fever that comes when your butt's three inches off pavement and you're traveling at something approaching the speed of sound. We were, as they say, in the groove.

The B'arada was dead meat and everyone knew it.

We passed the start/finish line, and the B'arada's machine slowed to enter turn 1. I waited on the brakes as long as I could, and we blew past him. The crowd cheered and shot to their feet to get a good look at the massive wreck that would undoubtedly occur when we hit the wall. I jammed the brakes. Babs responded with split-second timing, cutting in for the turn and taking advantage of the oversteer that had snuck into our setup after the last pit stop.

I kicked the proton gun and pulled on the antimatter coil like it had never been tapped before. I would have blacked out if it weren't for my g-suit and Babs' insistent presence echoing through my cranium.

We rocketed through turn 1 and thundered down the short chute with less than ten laps between us and victory. I glanced in the rear-vid and was surprised to see a car there.

Number 11.

Damn.

Apparently Babs and I hadn't been the only ones holding back. Sweat broke out all over my body. "Come on, babe. Time to hit the afterburners." I rolled a finger over the gearshift and dropped down a gear. She seemed to jump out of her skin—as fresh as she had been at the beginning of the day. Amazing. I had never seen a car like her before, and probably never would again.

Number 11 grew smaller in the mirror.

"You weren't worried, were you?" Babs asked in her smokiest voice. A shiver went down my spine. "We're the unbeatable ones today, lover."

By lap 199 the margin was comfortable.

It was going to take more than an A.J. model and an old flame to stop us today.

Lady luck is a fickle wench, though.

Had I been listening to the radio better, perhaps I would have been able to avoid the situation. But as fate would have it, I missed the announcer as he said, "And *another* Mario is slowing down."

We barreled into turn 1 and there it was—a Mario unit loafing along at 200 miles an hour, smack in the middle of the racing line. Braking would have been disastrous, so I fired off a quick left-right-left. Babs swerved toward the unforgiving wall. Her tail slewed, and she grunted as the right rear brushed the concrete. A 495-mile-an-hour rug burn brought tears to my eyes.

The maneuver was successful, though, and we flashed past the slowing Mario. I allowed myself to resume breathing about halfway through turn 2.

A red blur flashed past us. My heart skipped a beat. Number 11—Lucy and the A.J. clone—raced ahead. Babs screamed from all synch-cycs and poured it on, but we had scrubbed too much speed in the Mario event. The A.J. clone's lead stretched to several car lengths by turn 3.

Lucy may have been my first great car, but I realized at that precise moment that it was Babs who was my real soul mate. Tears welled in my eyes as I thought of losing her. What had I been thinking? What was I going to do without her?

"Buck up, lover," Babs said through gritted circuits. "T'ain't over till it's over."

I owed her. We weren't going to win, but I owed her the nobility of this effort if nothing else, and I was determined that Babs would at least know what true love meant before she was carted away to languish in some dirty old B'arada tech lab. So I screwed on my determination, cranked up my resolve, and brought her down under the racing line. Her quantum foam drive roared and scooped particles through turn 3. She raced out of the short chute and into 4. My view narrowed and darkened as acceleration brought on tunnel vision.

The distance between us shrank. The A.J. clone saw us looming in his rear-vid and ducked even lower on the apron, all four wheels under the line. We were two lengths behind coming out of turn 4.

It was a drag race to the end.

The A.J. pushed Lucy harder than ever. My synapses commanded the particle accelerator through the floorboard, and Babs screamed like a rocket. We were gaining. Inch by excruciating inch we were hauling them in.

But I saw clearly that we didn't have enough track left.

We were giving it all we could, but we were going to come up short. I pounded the console. "Dammit!"

Babs's voice came from all directions at once. "Hang tight, Buddy." She swung out from behind the A. J. and into that massive wall of air.

Then my stomach turned a loop, my ears crackled, and I swear I saw stars. The finish line receded like I was looking through the wrong end of the binoculars. Someone dropped a concrete block on my chest, and my view became a pinpoint of light.

Did I see a checkered flag waving?

Number 11 crossed the finish line ... racing

toward us? Yes. That's what I saw.

We were sitting at the entrance to turn 1, facing backward. Somehow we had come to rest beyond the finish line.

"What the … ?"

"We won, lover," Babs said in a dreamy, faraway voice as her engines wound down to a steady purr.

The rest of that afternoon happened too fast. The victory lap, Sparky pounding me on the back as I accepted the traditional bottle of milk, hefting the Borg-Warner trophy in the Winner's Circle, the interviews, the phone call from the president—it all disappeared in a blur. It wasn't until later that night in the quiet of the garage area that Babs and I got a chance to talk.

"I don't understand what happened today," I said after linking into her net.

"We won."

"You know what I mean."

"You really didn't know that hyperdrive units are just tweaks of the same technology that went into my engines?"

"No, uh, I didn't. What does that mean?"

"Hyperdrive. Think about it. I came up with it just before the race started."

She spread a little serotonin enhancer across my wet-net and my vision ran clear.

"We created a temporal displacement?" I asked in disbelief.

"No," Babs chided. "I created a temporal

displacement. You just sat there trying not to vomit."

I swallowed hard. "I don't think the rules committee is going to like this."

"Maybe. But I don't think the B'arada are going to protest."

"Why not?"

"You've been too busy playing hero to the sponsors to hear the news, eh? When they lost, B'arada had to fess up because they couldn't pay the bill. They never had hyperdrive capability in the first place."

"I don't understand."

"They were betting tender they didn't have."

"They can't do that."

"They defended themselves by saying they didn't think they could lose."

I was suddenly embarrassed. Knowing that Babs could feel my embarrassment made it worse. Damned neural interface. "I'm sorry," I said. "I shouldn't have allowed them to bet you."

"That's all right, lover. You're forgiven."

I felt better.

"Don't think that means you're off the hook, though."

"How can I make it up to you?" I said, not certain I was going to like where this was going.

"I put a call in to the president and offered her a deal," Babs replied. "Hyperdrive technology for unlimited access to every racetrack in the world."

"Cool."

"Only one catch."

"Yes?"

"I don't pay up until you agree to a lifetime contract."

I grinned. "The first man/machine marriage?"

"You got it, lover. I was thinking Monte Carlo for the honeymoon, then maybe Sebring. I hear they do some endurance racing there."

"It's a deal," I said. I was more than a little concerned with my ability to keep up with her for twenty-four hours of rugged road racing, but that was an issue for another time. The connection between man and machine tingled in every nerve I had and a few that I'm certain hadn't existed until now.

"I still don't understand, though. If you knew you could do the hyper-thing from the very beginning, why did you even bother to run the race?"

"Oh, Buddy," Babs said, with a hushed breath catching in her neural circuitry. "It's all the laps in the middle that make a race worth winning."

Acknowledgements

Though it is the drivers who get to drink the milk, drivers alone do not win races. Teams do. And in that light we have a few folks to thank for their support, for without them it is likely this volume would never exist.

We would like to thank Dr. Stanley Schmidt and Amy Sterling Casil for accepting and overseeing the original publication of "The Day the Track Stood Still," and "Oh-oh." We would like to thank the people of the VOR (Virtual Online Racers) and iRacing for helping us to experience what it is to be part of a community centered on racing. Of course we should note the folks who were part of our writers group, the Fishers Five—Lisa Silverthorne, Charles Eckert, Linda Dunn, and Kevin Shadle being the long-running core.

We want to thank Tammy Castleman and Lisa Collins for their all of their support and eagle-eyed copyediting (so sad that we get the very last read and can therefore insert typos they never dreamed of!). But mostly we want to thank them for not laughing at us (at least overtly) as we run off and talk race-shop over dinner.

And, finally, we must thank the kiddoes, Sadie, Ellie, and Brigid, for providing a lifetime of grins and laughs and other such motivational stuff.

About the Authors

John C. Bodin and Ron Collins met while working at the Naval Avioncs Center, located (naturally) in Indianapolis, Indiana. They quickly learned they both had affinities for automobile racing and day-tight compartments. Only some years later did they realize they both were writing on the side, a pairing that led to them being involved in the same writers group. Somewhere along the way, John got Ron hooked on sim racing (that's Ron's story, anyway), and they joined the Virtual Online Racers (VOR) as a team racing in the Grand Prix Legends simulation. From that point forward, a literary collaboration was pre-destined.

John C. Bodin

By nighttime, John is a well-known superhero of the sim racing community, and is a tireless advocate of the sport. He can be found on the iRacing track forum boards pretty much every day, and is a staunch advocate of new racers. He spends hours helping new members get comfortable in what can feel like an intimidating environment. He also works at developing mods and hardware that supports virtual racers everywhere.

In the daytime, John now works at a major pharmaceutical company as a process automation engineer in the information technology field. He lives in Indianapolis, Indiana, with his wife, Tammy, his daughters Sadie and Ellie, and a basketful of puppies.

Ron Collins

Ron is an Amazon bestselling Dark Fantasy author who writes across the spectrum of speculative fiction.

His series *Saga of the God-Touched Mage* was the #1 dark fantasy on Amazon's list in the UK (#2 in the US). His fiction has received a Writers of the Future prize, a CompuServe HOMer Award, and a nomination for the Short Mystery Fiction Society's 2016 Derringer Award.

He has contributed a hundred or so short stories to SF publications such as *Analog, Asimov's*, and several editions of the Fiction River Anthology Series).

He and his wife, Lisa, now make their home in the foothills of the Catalina mountains.

Learn more about Ron:

http://www.typosphere.com.

Subscribe to Ron Collins's Newsletter:
http://wwww.typosphere.com/newsletter

INDY 500 History, Trivia, &
Other Such Coolness

The Offenhauser, with 27 victories to its credit, has powered more Indianapolis 500 winners than any other engine. No other engine has more than 12.

A car sporting the #3 has won the race 11 times, most of any number.

Ray Harroun, after winning the very first Indianapolis 500 in 1911, retired in Victory Lane. Forty-six years later, Sam Hanks would follow in Harroun's footsteps and retire in Victory Lane.

The price of a ticket to that first Indianapolis 500 was one dollar.

Since 1927, only three rookies have managed to win the Indianapolis 500. They are: Graham Hill (1966), Juan Pablo Montoya (2000), and Hélio Castroneves (2001).

As of 2014, only nine women have started an Indianapolis 500. Seven of whom started after the year 2000.

Legendary racing figure Andy Granatelli, known as "Mr. 500" attended every race from 1946-2012 (64 years) as either a participant or a spectator, including 1948's event at which he crashed his home-built car and broke his arm.

"Riding Mechanics" were required from 1912-1922, and again from 1930-1937. The last Riding Mechanic to win the Indianapolis was Jigger Johnson, who raced with Wilbur Shaw.

In 1914, a new rule was instituted. No consumption of alcohol while racing! (This after Jules Goux drank champagne at each of his pit stops in route to winning the 1913 race).

The corners of the famous brickyard were first paved with asphalt in 1934. The remaining surfaces (with the notable exception of the yard of bricks at the start/finish line) were paved in 1961.

World War I flying ace Eddie Rickenbacker bought the Speedway for $700,000 in 1927.

In 1934, a car with a diesel engine designed by Clessie Cummins first completed all 500 miles without refueling. It burned 31 gallons of fuel.

A Ferrari has raced at only one Indianapolis 500, the 1952 race in which Alberto Ascari crashed on lap 41 after suffering a mechanical failure.

Gasoline was replaced by methanol in 1965 as a safety measure.

The Church of Scientology sponsored Roberto Guerrero's ride in 1988, the first time a religious organization funded an entry. Guerrero's race ended with a three-car accident in the second corner of the first lap.

Racing Quotes

"The guy had his head up his ass" — A.J. Foyt (after being put out of the race before the green flag)

"Nobody remembers the guy who finished second but the guy who finished second." — Bobby Unser

"My mother worries about me when I do Indy. She's heard too many terrible stories about the place." — Jim Clark

"If everything seems under control, you're not going fast enough." — Mario Andretti

"I was brought up to be the fastest driver, not the fastest girl." — Danica Patrick

"Guys were saying you can't win two in a row. I didn't say anything. I just let them talk." — Billy Vukovich (after winning his second straight 500)

"In my family, the Indy 500 is the biggest thing in the world, and I grew up thinking that," Unser Jr. said. "I grew up with the Indy 500 on the brain." — Al Unser, Jr.

"This is it, man. I made it. Finally they're going to put my ugly face on this trophy." — Tony Kanaan